BACKtrack

HAROLD JOHNSON

thistledown press

Thistledown Press Ltd.
410 @nd Avenue North
Saskatoon, Saskatchewan, S7K 2C3
www.thistledownpress.com

Library and Archives Canada Cataloguing in Publication

Johnson, Harold, 1957–
Back track / Harold Johnson.

ISBN 978-1-894345-85-9

I. Title.

PS8569.O328B32 2005   C813'.6   C2005-904845-X

Cover painting: *Spirit Dancer* by Jim Poitras
Cover and book design by Jackie Forrie
Printed and bound in Canada on acid-free paper

Canada Council   Conseil des Arts
for the Arts   du Canada

ARTS BOARD

Canadian   Patrimoine
Heritage   canadien

Thistledown Press gratefully acknowledges the financial assistance of the Canada Council for the Arts, the Saskatchewan Arts Board, and the Government of Canada through the Canada Book Fund for its publishing program.

I dedicate this book to my loving spouse Joan who heard the story as it was revealed to us. To my daughters, Sarah, Alita and Harmony; my sons Ray and Mike, my granddaughter Elizabeth and in memory of my mother, my first teacher of storytelling.

To Rod McDermott and James Auger who helped me develop as a storyteller, and a big special thanks to Seán Virgo who was very honest with me through the editing process.

CONTENTS

Northwind

Northwind rattled the snow from the boughs of the frozen Spruce; shook loose the white clusters and sent them tumbling. The crisp boughs waved in the wind. Motion usually indicates life. Jimmy knew that Spruce was alive and asleep. He also knew that Northwind brought death; or rather that Northwind came to carry away the living. Life and Death; the pretence of life and the living dead, cold thoughts drifted in and out of his mind.

Northwind found its way into Jimmy's parka, chilling his throat and chest. He resisted pulling the zipper higher until the cold began to reach lower and bring a chill to his entirety, as though the blood flowing through his heart had cooled.

With his zipper cold under his chin, Jimmy felt constrained. He tried loosening the shoulder straps on his packsack for the freedom. But that only caused the pack to ride lower. He snugged the straps to their original notch so that the steel traps in the packsack did not bounce against his kidneys.

Jimmy quickened his pace. His left snowshoe caught on a crust of snow and snagged him. He stumbled and caught himself with a curse. "Slow down, relax." He stopped at his own inner command, looked up and back down the trail at the brilliant sun in the Southern sky guarded by equally bright sun dogs, which flared from horizon to mid sky.

Without conscious thought, Jimmy's environment informed him that the day was half-over and that it was extremely cold. What did make it into Jimmy's consciousness was his danger. A hurried mistake now would leave him as dead and stiff as the few animals he found in his traps.

Jimmy rationalized his position. He had three traps yet to check; maybe set some of the traps in the packsack if he found animal sign and a likely spot to set. If he did not set any more traps, he would likely be home in an hour. Plenty of time to cut firewood and skin and stretch the frozen weasel in his packsack. Then nothing until dark and bed.

Jimmy had been driven by the noise and confusion of town to the solitude of the trapline. Now that he was alone he sometimes found it hard. Days and weeks of silence unbroken by television and traffic, but also devoid of laughter, pulled at his mind during the empty times. He kept himself busy from daylight until dark, sustaining himself, and trying to outsmart animals with bait, steel and snares.

"Well! Well! Well! What have we here?" Jimmy came out of his dark thoughts at the sight of a silver fox standing amid scattered boughs. Fox's foreleg was caught in a steel trap and he had demolished the carefully constructed set. "Not as smart as you thought, eh?" Jimmy removed his snowshoes. "Got yourself caught in my Martin trap. Well you're not worth as much but you'll do. Hold still now and I'll kill you quick. Give me a hard time; we'll take longer." Jimmy smashed Fox's skull with the back of an axe.

Jimmy removed his thick mitts and compressed the spring of the trap. As he began to remove it from Fox's leg, Fox bit. A long sharp canine tooth went through the back of his hand. He grabbed Fox by the scruff of the neck, yanked his hand free from Fox's jaw, grabbed the axe and using the blunt end made sure Fox was dead.

There would not be any free time this evening. By the time he got to the cabin, skinned and stretched Fox and patched his hand, it would be well past dark. In his rush Jimmy forgot to put down tobacco and thank Grandmother Earth for her generosity.

Hangover

Charles opened his eyes and immediately shut them. Daylight burned into his brain. Consciousness was the last thing that Charles desired. He slowly, painfully rose. Maybe there was a beer left over from the night before. All he found were empties. A promising half-full bottle on the table dashed his hopes by containing a cigarette butt.

Charles abandoned his search for alcohol and began looking for something to smoke. All of the packages he found littered on the floor or on the table contained only foil. The need in his centre increased in volume until his ears rang. The need felt like an empty spot. An empty spot that grew larger, until it threatened to make Charles disappear. Fill the hole or vanish. Pour alcohol into the void, fill it with smoke, do anything to make it go away, be whole.

Charles frantically searched through the empty rooms. There was nothing to drink in the fridge or anywhere else. There were no forgotten bottles, caps intact. There were no joints on the table or hidden in an empty cigarette package.

Charles' wallet wasn't in his hip pocket. Not that he'd expected to find much money in it. He checked the couch he had been sleeping on. Not under the cushions. He stood then, trying to remember the details of the night before. He had seventy dollars in his wallet when he walked into the bar. The rest was blank. Charles could not recall the first drink that he must have had. Seventy dollars gone and he could not even remember the beginning of the good time that he set out to find.

The empty spot swallowed some of Charles's lungs until he had trouble breathing. It was going to make him disappear. Charles was going to vanish from the inside out. He searched again through the cupboards, fruitlessly, for anything with alcohol. No vanilla extract. He thought of drinking bleach, but could not imagine that it would fill the void. He checked the bathroom for aftershave and was rewarded with a bottle of Old Spice that sounded with a swirl when he shook it. Charles pried off the lid and poured the contents into his mouth. He swallowed quickly to avoid the taste. The white bottle with the sailboat only held enough for a taste; soapy and bitter; not nearly enough to fill the need.

Charles lay on the couch. The 30/30 Winchester barrel rested against the empty spot. He closed his eyes and pulled the trigger. The force of the rifle blast lifted him off the cushions as it slammed through Charles' empty spot. The one hundred and seventy grain shell nicked Charles' lower right lung and exited at two thousand feet per second, barely missing his spine. He had a broken rib and minor injuries to his lung, chest and back.

He sat up amazed at the power of a rifle. The empty feeling was gone. Had he killed it or scared it away? Charles walked to the door. A thought that he was only a spirit caused him to look back at the couch to see if his dead body was there. It wasn't. Charles lived, breathed, walked and finally sat on the steps outside of the blue and white reserve house, looking down the gravel road at the children running toward him drawn by the rifle's bang.

The nurses were carrying arms and legs as they walked quickly past the door to the hospital room. Charles lay strapped to the bed. They were going to come and cut him to pieces and carry him away. Charles struggled against the straps. The pain in his centre stole his strength or he would have snapped the straps and run.

The horror had been there as long as Charles could remember. The hospital horror. He knew that all that was needed for the horror to go away was a drink. One drink and he would be okay. The horror would stop. The empty spot had taken over Charles. He hadn't vanished. Instead he had come to this place of horror. The empty spot was not empty. It was filled with demons.

Charles could hear the hooves of the boss demon on the crisp tiles of the hospital floor. He clenched his eyelids hard using his cheek and forehead muscles to force them shut. The Devil himself walked in the sterile room. Charles could not shut his ears to the clatter of hooves on the floor. He screamed to drown the sound. The pain in his centre stole his strength and the scream came out a pitiful whimper. Now the Devil was shaking a half full bottle of whiskey. Charles could hear the liquid against the glass.

"Open your eyes, Charlie. Come on buds, have a little drink with me."

The Devil swished the whiskey and Charles screamed again. A nurse came in to check the straps and the Devil vanished.

"Relax Charlie, it's just the DTs, they won't last — relax now so you don't break the stitches."

Charles quit. He was beaten. He kept his eyes closed but the tears forced themselves through and emerged triumphant upon his cheeks, rolled openly back and down toward his ears. He shook his head to clear them, then gave up and let himself cry. This was the lowest he had ever been. Beaten, alone, with no one left to blame but himself. He was nothing more than sediment in the bottom of a nearly empty bottle. The pain in Charles' centre pulsated in rhythm with his sobs.

Shadow Man

Henry ran across the open space, up the steps onto the airplane, found a place to sit and mumbled apologies to Judge Friesen and the prosecutor. Friesen's face disclosed his annoyance at the legal aid lawyer who had the audacity to make a provincial court judge wait.

"Fuck him," Henry thought to himself. "The asshole doesn't have a clue." To Friesen, the Resource Officers and RCMP were the epitome of truth. Anyone who contradicted the testimony of either was lying. Police and Resource Officers did not lie. Not in Friesen's travelling circus.

The plane made its way down the runway in preparation. Henry stared out the window at the passing pines beyond the tarmac. He had seen this show many times before. This was his second year and already he was tired.

Friesen and the prosecutor were carrying on their normal patter. Weather predictions, flight times, lunch in Creighton during recess. Should they have the buffet or ask an RCMP officer for a ride into Flin Flon for a real meal. The prosecutor asked Henry for his opinion. Henry answered with a shrug. It did not matter.

The plane was airborne with a leap, gaining altitude over the pines, now above frozen Lac La Ronge, rising higher, turning East and levelling off. Henry wished he were heading West, to the trapline where James still had not heard that Charles had shot himself.

Calm steady James; this news would shake him up. His little brother Charles had shot himself. Henry wondered at his own position. This was one hell of a day to be a lawyer. One of his brothers was in a Southern hospital; the other was beyond modern telecommunications. Charles had phoned his older brother Edward at the mining camp, but Edward was too busy making money to be very concerned.

Friesen tapped Henry's knee.

"I heard about Charles, damn shame. How's he doing?"

"Last I heard he wasn't in serious condition. Thanks for asking."

Henry brusquely turned back to the window. How did the asshole find out so fast? Of course the RCMP would have known and they certainly were not models of discretion, at least among their own. The brotherhood of prosecutor, Judge, officers and clerks shared information. They were an island community in a sea of Northern Indians. In their minds they were the defenders of right, stationed temporarily in the North to accomplish their mission of bringing order to the unwashed masses.

They all dreamed of the day when they would be posted South. The North was their ticket to accelerated promotion. They would return to civilization with stories of deviance. They had seen the truth of the North. Some would become "experts", advisors and consultants, telling government how to manage Northern affairs. As far as Henry was concerned, not one of them truly understood what it was like to live in the North.

Henry stared out the window and tried to concentrate on the past, but it was not a place where Henry found solace. He had grown up on the wrong side of the reserve line. His youth had been a mix of drugs, alcohol and violence. His future did not hold much hope either. As a legal aid lawyer he would never become one of the wealthy elite of his profession. He was paid less than the prosecutor who worked for the same ultimate government employer. The best Henry could hope for if he stayed on his present career path was to become a judge. One look at Friesen and Henry knew he had to change paths.

Henry watched the shadow of the airplane glide across the frozen lake. The snow and ice reflected the sun's brightness with a double intensity that flashed through the cold air between the plane and its shadow. Henry imagined himself on the lake, maybe ice fishing. The skimming shadow reached the shore and his imagination was carried into the trees. The shadow contorted as it ruffled against the rough surface of black Spruce and muskeg, reformed itself as it sped across a frozen river and lost its shape again in the trees. Henry saw himself as the shadow. Just skimming life. Travelling too fast to ever fully experience a place, never touching more than the surface of the North. The files he was assigned today were like that. Quick motions before Friesen after a fifteen-minute interview with the accused.

Henry picked up his pen. Now he was official. Peter Rabbitskin continued to talk. "She doesn't look after the kids all the time; her mom keeps them lots. I should have to pay her mom."

"Does her mother want a portion of the child support?"

"I don't know. I never talk to her."

"Your wife's petition for child support does not claim child care expenses. I don't think we should mention it. I do not want to put anything extra in Judge Friesen's mind. Your wife . . . " Henry flipped through the file on the table, found the petition and the *Style of Cause* naming the parties . . . "Joyce, is asking for sole custody of the children but does not mention access. What sort of schedule do you want for visiting your children?"

"Whenever. I can visit them when they're not in school, but she won't let me in the house."

"You have to exercise access on a regular basis at your own residence. Judge Friesen will take her position into consideration when determining access. He's not about to make an access order that might result in domestic violence. I am not saying there will be a confrontation if you exercise access at Joyce's residence but that will be in Judge Friesen's mind."

"Where you from?" Peter asked a distracted Henry who looked up from his pad. Friesen had granted him fifteen minutes to interview Peter and he did not want to waste any of it on immaterial visiting.

"La Ronge." Henry answered.

"You sound like you're from the city."

Henry sat back and looked at Peter really for the first time. Here was a man in his early thirties. Dressed typically poor and practical. Black hair cut by his sister. A dark face, darker than was becoming typical in the Caucasian-influenced North. Brown eyes that showed kindness, a kindness that surprised Henry. It was a reversal of purpose. Henry imagined himself as the people's champion and here was a man whose eyes and voice seemed to express pity — or was it contempt?

"You look like an Indian but you sound white."

Before Henry could respond, not that he had a response, the court clerk knocked on the door to the witness interview room. "Judge Friesen wants to know if you are ready to proceed." She announced.

"I haven't had fifteen minutes yet."

"Well, he wants you back in the courtroom."

By the time Henry returned and explained to the impatient Judge Friesen that he was not prepared to proceed and returned to continue the interview, five more of his fifteen minutes had elapsed.

Henry stood behind the defence counsel's table instead of in his usual spot beside it. He wanted to be seen standing beside his client, a show of solidarity. "Peter wants to exercise his right to access, but Peter does not have a residence of his own." He was using Peter's name excessively to personalize him to Judge Friesen.

"Peter intends to build a larger cabin on his trapline and desires to have his children with him during school breaks and during the summer."

This last was a complete fabrication on Henry's part. Peter's trapline was almost impossible to get to during the summer because of the same muskeg that made it fur rich.

Peter sat at the table at the front of the courtroom. He kept his eyes lowered, finding interesting things on the table. Hearing his name was an odd experience. He had told Henry his name was Mule. He had not said it was the name he had been called by exclusively since he was seven and had been seen by most of the community pulling home a large toboggan full of firewood. Most of the people in the courtroom were not certain who this Indian lawyer was talking about. They did not know that Mule's birth certificate, archived at the Department of Health in Regina declared that he was Peter Allen Rabbitskin. Henry's repeated use of Mule's official name generated a sense of unreality that made the court seem doubly foreign and wrong.

Henry had another reason for standing behind the defence counsel's table. It gave him something to hold onto. He did not know why, despite his experience in courtrooms and before judges, an occasional panic attack would hit him. This was one of those times. Perhaps it came from not being prepared, or perhaps from being over prepared. Henry kept talking. He heard the nervousness in his voice; the higher pitch, the quickened speech, the words in a tumult. He forced himself to slow down. Deliberately he stopped for a few heartbeats and flipped pages forward then back, and continued. He wanted to sit down, but he knew that if he did he would never win this battle with nerves. Henry stood, and forced himself to keep talking. Every motion, every gesture became deliberate as Henry finished his presentation and sat to wait for Judge Friesen's decision.

Dreams

The wind blew the snow past Jimmy's only window. He turned his bannock in the bacon grease, toward the light to determine the degree of brown. Breakfast of bacon and fried bannock; Jimmy was being decadent this morning. Near blizzard conditions meant that he would spend the day in or near the cabin. Bacon for breakfast was a luxury that Jimmy indulged in only rarely. He had calculated how many breakfasts were left in the slab before he had cut this morning's share. He knew that the old lonely feeling would creep up on him. He intentionally began the day with bacon to pamper himself. If he started in a good mood he might be able to sustain the feeling longer into the coming day.

Jimmy thought about what work he might indulge in today while he savoured his breakfast. The pelts he had accumulated so far could be sorted and checked. There were few that needed any substantial work. Some would require wiping down as they dried. There was still a good pile of firewood outside; no need to cut any more; no sense in hauling any more water; he did not have storage capacity beyond the two large pails that were already nearly full. Jimmy would wash his dishes, clean the bite on his hand, sweep the floor, wash his clothes and the old bandages in the same aluminum basin that he had used for the dishes, hang the clothes inside the cabin to dry, make another pot of coffee. The desire for a human voice hit him hard while he sat looking out the window at the blowing snow. He put down his cup of coffee, drew in a deep breath, went to the door for his parka and boots and went out into the storm.

The driving snow stung Jimmy's exposed face. The wind sucked his breath away. The drifted snow tangled his feet. He drove himself forward, face into the wind, forcing each leg in turn to rise and crunch down into the snow. He was off the trail because he was not going anywhere. He was just walking. Not a gentle stroll, but a deliberate endurance exercise designed to drive the wanting from his mind.

Jimmy knew his weakness. It was loneliness. He either conquered it or submitted to its power. Loneliness would eventually drive Jimmy back to the noise and confusion of town. The longer he held out, the more fur he would take back with him. The more fur he sold, the more money he would have. The more money . . . he would decide what to do with the proceeds when he had them in his pocket.

The trapline isolation soothed Jimmy's mind for a while. He became peaceful and quiet out here. Then loneliness would pull him back to town where he would become agitated by the noise and commotion once more and again flee back to the safety of the trapline. Jimmy lived a cycle of town and trapline that was influenced by the seasons but was determined by his emotions.

Jimmy's strategy was to change whatever he was doing in order to change whatever he was thinking. He found that some activities were better than others for avoiding particular thoughts. Making coffee got rid of lustful thoughts. Playing cards removed violent thoughts. Hard physical work removed loneliness like sweat washes away grime.

The phrase "open for me Gladys" came embodied in a naked image. It slammed into Jimmy's mind as he walked through the wind and snow. The image moved, spread naked legs and unfolded its arms outward. Jimmy allowed the phrase and the image to echo and unfold in his mind.

He felt warm. He pulled back his parka hood and knelt in the snow. Jimmy lowered his head and with the viral thought still growing he sank his face into the snow until his entire head was covered.

Gladys kept typing as she spread her thighs to ease the moist swollen feeling. "Jimmy, hurry your ass home," she thought. Her eyes read the Director of Social Services report to the Minister; her fingers found the computer keys in rapid succession. The words of the report did not register in her mind. Gladys' mind was full of Jimmy. How he walked, that long determined stride that she had trouble keeping up with. Jimmy's laugh that always came from his stomach. He threw his head back and let the laugh roar up and out.

Gladys squeezed her thighs back together, tight. The pressure rose from her thighs through her vagina and upward to behind her breasts. Gladys rolled her shoulders back to make room for the pressure. She willed it to subside and it settled in her buttocks as she lifted slightly from the chair. "Aw, Jimmy you're not even here and you have me wiggling."

Wetiko

Jimmy's brain hurt. It was not a headache in any normal sense. The entire inside of his skull burned. Jimmy unzipped his sleeping bag and rolled out of bed. He fumbled with the coal oil lamp, knocking the globe onto the table, cursed his clumsiness. He only had one globe and if he broke it he would be without light. Jimmy struck a match to the lamp wick. The pale yellow light showed him his leather medicine bag hanging on the wall. Jimmy pulled on the drawstrings, pulled out a short piece of root, bit off a piece, bitter on his tongue. He found a sharp knife to slice the remainder down into shavings. While Jimmy waited for the shavings to boil, he sat on the bed and held his head in his hands. The heat from the over-stuffed stove, the loud crackle of the fire drilled into his skull. He chewed hard on the root waiting for it to dull the pain. Endurance, hold on for as long as possible and when about to give up ask *Can I handle more?* Look inside and see if there is anything left. Jimmy concentrated on holding still to out wait the pain. The chewed root had no effect, and it was long after the remainder had boiled, cooled, and been swallowed that the pain subsided to a sting and Jimmy could relax.

Jimmy cursed having stuck his head in the snow. Now he had a cold of the brain he concluded. He remembered the torment when he had a cold in his testicles. How he had limped to the clinic ashamed because he was certain that he had a venereal disease. That torment had lasted for several days. Jimmy thought about his traps. He hadn't checked them the last two days because of the storm. Now he would be cabin-bound because of his foolishness. Any fur would be chewed by mice, or ripped apart by Raven or Owl.

Jimmy collapsed from the exhaustion of enduring the pain in his skull. The next morning the pain was totally gone. Not only that, but Jimmy awoke filled with hunger and energy. He ate hurriedly and surprised himself by trotting while checking his traps. Most of his thoughts were joyous as he walked quickly or trotted. Jimmy talked aloud to the trees and birds. Saying "good morning" and inquiring about their well-being. He laughed when Raven cawed a reply. "Because you haven't eaten my catch, come by the cabin later and I'll set you a table of the most delectable rare Martin." And he did. Jimmy found a square of plywood and generously used a few of his precious nails to secure it to a stump. A fine table for a neighbour. Jimmy enjoyed the humour of setting a table for a scavenger that found many meals in trashcans and along the highways.

The next days Jimmy hardly thought at all. His mood was ecstatic. He laughed when he found fur in his traps. He joked with Raven or Owl when he found an animal damaged by one of the birds. He asked Tree, "Who was eating here when I was gone?" and laughed when he received no reply, "Oh, sorry, didn't mean to bother you while you were asleep".

Jimmy ate twice his normal amount and enjoyed every mouthful. He had taken to eating mostly meat and barely cooked it. He wondered why he hadn't eaten it that way before. The meat juices were much better when they held the wild flavour. Maybe Raven knew more about eating than people thought. Rare was best.

Jimmy woke from the cold dream world and caught his breath. He sat up and looked around the cabin in the dark. He didn't notice that his night vision was exceptional. More on his mind was the dream. She had offered him a human arm to taste, and he had enjoyed the tenderness. He still tasted the juices in his mouth and wiped at his chin, then checked his hand to see if there really was blood. There wasn't. The dream had been real, though. Jimmy could still see the woman, tall, slim with a prance to her walk. Jimmy had wanted to have sex with the woman. He ate the flesh she offered to impress her. He wanted her to see him as a man, a man unafraid of anything.

He added wood to the fire. He felt chilled to the core. As Jimmy walked around the cabin, pulled on a sweater and waited for the stove to throw warmth, the dream faded. The brightness of the image dimmed. The sharp of her voice mellowed. What was it she had said? Jimmy tried to remember. "Here". No, there was more. What was it? He could not remember. Had she said "Here", or had she said something else. Maybe she used the Cree word *Na*. The further away from the dream the less important it seemed. Jimmy opened the door and looked out at the sky. The handle of the Big Dipper indicated that it was a couple of hours to daybreak. The night was unusually bright. Jimmy decided to go check his traps. The dream hardly seemed real at all.

The Sun began to show bright in the Southeast, pink and peach as Jimmy trotted, packsack bouncing on his back. Checking traps in the dark added a dimension to his experience.

She came to Jimmy again the next night. Her hair billowed loose in the dream wind. She turned around, making a circle before approaching to stand in front of him. Jimmy looked into her smiling face. It was a face of confidence, daring. She needed no words to tell Jimmy as she raised her arm to his face. Jimmy knew. He tasted her flesh, sank his teeth into the softness, let the juices fill him. Again and again Jimmy fed his hunger on her flesh. Snapped a bone and sucked out the marrow. The feeding was frenzy. The juices went straight to his brain. They filled Jimmy with power. His vision cleared until all was crystal and bright. His ears popped, and he could hear. He could hear the drum beat of life. The heart thump. The music that accompanied the beauty. The light and the sounds danced together. Jimmy danced, a grass dance, swirling to the light and the drum. He did not trample the grass. He danced between the blades; he danced with the grass. He was grass and more. He was alive.

Jimmy woke. Light poured into the cabin through the window. Bright sunlight that filled and pressurized the tiny space. Light so bright that it burned. Jimmy hung a heavy wool blanket over the window.

Jimmy knew he was not snow blind. He knew what that was like. This was not the same. The light of day did not burn and sting. His eyes did not water uncontrollably. Yet that is what Jimmy told himself. "I am sunblind," he repeated to himself. He refused to admit that he was afraid of light. Jimmy would not admit fear of anything. Those *Wetiko* stories were just to frighten children. Flesh eating dreams were just dreams. Jimmy repeated to himself "I am sunblind, that is all. In a few days it will go away. Until then I will just have to check my traps after dark." He did not explain how he could see in the dark and he did not ask.

Anonymity

"Hi, my name is Felix and I am an alcoholic."

"Hello Felix," the circle ritually responded to the opening statement.

"It took me a long time to admit that. That I'm an alcoholic. I sometimes wish I'd admitted it earlier. I wouldn't have wasted all those years when I was drunk. I'm really happy to've found my way to AA. I've been sober now for better'n three years and they've been the best three years of my life. When I was drinking I was miserable and I drank to get happy. The more I drank the more miserable I became. At first I blamed everyone else, my wife, my boss. If only they'd leave me alone. It was their fault I was miserable. My excuse for drinking was to have a good time. I needed to have a good time because everyone around me was bringing me down. The problem was that I was a miserable drunk. Now being sober, taking one day at a time, working on the steps, working on myself, I'm a lot happier. Oh, life isn't perfect, my wife and my boss haven't changed, but now I don't run away to the bottle. Instead I call my sponsor when it gets rough and I talk to my higher power when the urge to drink comes along."

Felix continued the story that he had told to this circle every week. They did not mind; they appreciated the variations.

Charles could not commit. This was too strange of a place for him to talk about the Devil. When his turn came around to share, Charles said "Thank you," and passed. He did not admit his alcoholism, to them or to himself. He came to the Thursday evening meetings at the Friendship Centre to listen and learn. The stories fed the empty spot enough that he could live until the next week's meeting. But it was a circle of strangers, motivated only by their individual needs. Charles did not feel any guilt in his taking. The participants were there for themselves and so was he.

Charles looked down into his coffee cup. His wavy reflection stared back at him from the oily black surface. The face looked sad and hurt, it matched the soul. Felix continued to share his strategy of sobriety with the circle " . . . and my higher power is the Great Spirit." Charles abruptly looked up from his reflection and around the room of mostly white participants. It struck him as wrong to talk of the Great Spirit here in the tile and plaster room with fluorescent lights and clinical white ceiling. The Great Spirit belonged in Uncle Zach's sweat lodge of bent Willow with its earth floor. Charles drifted back to a peaceful time, visiting his great uncle in a warm sunny cabin, while Felix continued to talk about working the twelve steps of the program. Uncle Zach stirred a cup of tea.

"There's no wrong way to worship. All us Indians have a way to pray and if you travel around you'll see we pray pretty much the same everywhere. The Sioux to the South have a strong way to pray. They kept their culture and live it. To the North the Dene pray their way. The Saulteaux brought their understanding out West hundreds of years ago. We all pray the same way, just with our own understanding. The white man prays too and now the New Age people are looking at our way of praying. Like I said, there is no wrong way. If you want to pray with the Sioux, pray their way. If you pray with the Saulteaux, do like they do. We Cree have our way." Uncle Zach patted his green canvas pack. "It's the way of our Grandfathers and Grandmothers and it is a good way but it is not the only way. Don't ever go somewhere and tell people they're doing something wrong because they aren't doing it like us. That would be arrogant and we are humble people. Just don't mix things up. Don't mix Christian things with Cree things. Don't mix New Age ideas with what you learn here. If you mix these ways up, mix Cree with Saulteaux with Sioux with Jesus and crystals all you are going to do is mix yourself up."

Charles drank his warm coffee, tasted the smooth bitter black, felt it warm his centre and sat up straighter. Alcoholics Anonymous was a good place, but Charles was an Indian and Indians have good things too.

Edward threw a bag of Amex explosive over his shoulder and walked to the waiting Almac. There is no sunset underground. Raise mining has its own glory and history and bonus. In the early years, raise miners worked from wooden platforms that they carried piece by piece up wooden ladders and constructed sometimes over a hundred feet above the beginning level. From the platform they drilled overhead to extend the raise eight feet at a time. Drill a pattern of holes. Fill the holes with dynamite. Tear down the platform and ladders. Blast the round. Muck out the blasted rock with a shovel. Replace the ladders and platform and start again.

An Almac replaced the need to constantly build and tear down. It was a platform that travelled on a rail. As each round advanced upward, another section of rail was added. The Almac climbed and crawled down the rail powered by a pneumatic motor. The lives of the miners depended upon air pressure and the two-inch bull hose that fed air to the Almac motor, powered their drills, provided fresh air for them to breath and blew the powdered Amex explosive into the drill holes.

Raise mining always paid the highest bonus. It also cost the highest number of lives and injuries. Edward worked for the bonus, calculated seconds that added to minutes that added to production and the advancement of the raise and his bonus cheque. He wished the Almac would travel faster as it slowly climbed the single rail eighty feet to the waiting round. Four more good rounds this pay period should earn a bonus that would put him over the top. Two ex-wives, child support for two and Revenue Canada needed feeding. In the end Edward took home only a quarter of his pay cheque. Over the years he had forgotten the joy of work, put those feelings away and not brought them out. Work was about money. Hard work and hard money. When he was not calculating seconds, he was adding his bonus. The slow ride up and down the raise on the Almac gave ample time for thought. He no longer thought about the Almac jumping a worn track and tumbling down the raise to the muck pile. Those are greenhorn thoughts, like cave-ins and floods. Instead he thought about how to shave minutes from a short day. How to start the drill into the rock face without it slipping and sliding around before it bit. How to load the Amex explosive into the holes without leaving air spaces that might result in a misfire and more work the next round.

Edward let his mind drift momentarily to Charles. His brother was an idiot. Shooting himself over a woman. How stupid. Henry said that Lorna left La Ronge the day before Charles shot himself. Edward put the two together and came to the conclusion that Charles attempted suicide because Lorna left. Edward lived in a world of simplicity. Hard work equals more money. More money equals more everything. Charles shot himself because he was a weakling around women. Simple. Edward made an agreement with himself to stop in and see how Charles was doing and then went back to thinking about mining. Simple.

Edward enjoyed calculations. His soul was most at peace when he kept his mind working, or rather, he did not hear his soul's mourning when his mind was busy, when his body was busy.

"Just a couple nights left to this rotation and it's home sweet home eh, Ed?" Phil Miller wanted to talk.

"Uh huh." Edward didn't. They sat in the bus parked behind the mine and waited until exactly 7:00 AM when the bus would carry them back to the camp.

"Bin thinkin' 'bout this seven and seven rotation we're on." Phil tapped the metal lunch pail on his lap. "Seven days *in* — seven days *out*." Edward made no response. "Why do they call the time we spend here *in* and the time we spend at home *out*?" Edward didn't answer, so Phil did. "'Cause it's like jail. *In* jail and *out* of jail."

"Maybe."

"Come on. Don't you see it?"

"It's not so bad. Hell of a lot worse when we worked twenty-one in and seven out."

"I'm not saying it's better or worse. I'm just wondering why we use those words. In and out."

"Guess it has something to do with the plane. We fly *in* to camp and *out* to the world."

"That's what I'm sayin'. Why don't we call it flying *out* to work and *in* to the world."

"Got me."

Phil gave up. The bus driver boarded the bus and lurched it forward to begin the ride to the camp, breakfast and a day's sleep before both these miners would have to return to the mine for another night shift. Phil's thoughts were about one less day before he flew home to his family. Edward's were about how much work he would do tonight.

Bingo

Gladys looked up at the number board and down again at the Bingo cards, dabbed B–14 on five out of the nine cards she played. She'd decided to come to the hall with her Grandmother because she had nothing better to do. Television left her empty; she wanted to talk, not be talked to by the box that flashed and flittered cinematic nonsense. The hall was full of people dabbing cards, drinking coffee and praying for the number that would allow them to raise their hand in the air indicating a win. The conversation between games centred entirely upon how close the players had come to winning.

"Needed O–74 for the last three numbers".

"I wasn't even close."

Gladys kept quiet, looked at her *Nokom*, wishing she could go back to being a child again with *Nokom* taking care of all her little problems. *Nokom*, telling her about first woman, about her moon cycles and the old days. Gladys let her mind drift to the earlier time, the little reserve house, *Nokom*, and her and her little brother Jesse. *Nokom* had tried to send Jesse out with the men whenever she had a chance. "Go with Paul to cut wood. Help Jacob today." Jesse had resisted. He felt that he was being chased away. It was enough to be without parents, he complained to Gladys, now his *Nokom* chased him away.

Sadness grasped Gladys when she let her thoughts turn to Jesse. Maybe he would get things together in jail. He needed somewhere, she rationalized, to work out his anger.

Jesse had stood up to a boy larger than himself. It was over nothing, the way everything was. It was how a person stood or did not stand, or looked straight ahead or looked down. A fight could start with a look, a roll of the eye, and a fist would smash. Jail was about getting the hell out of bed in the morning, washing dishes, cleaning and working, jumping when yelled at, and never, never, being last or first. Find a middle place in everything and hold it. Whelan was bigger and louder and from the city. He hated Jesse, Jesse was sure, because Jesse was from the North and spoke Cree. No words were spoken in the exchange but both Jesse and Whelan knew how close they had come to fists and boots. Jesse held his place, stood straight and refused to look away. Whelan blinked first and strutted away.

Jesse hugged his pillow in the dark of the room that smelled like a hospital, like antiseptic, Mr. Clean and Dettol. He had no one to stand up to in the dark, no reason to be tough. He felt the tightness in his throat and the sting beneath his eyes and because no one was watching, because he was alone and no one cared, Jesse cried and Gladys felt the sadness and the loneliness.

"*Nokom*, do you want more tea?" Gladys found an excuse to leave the table.

"I can't watch your cards and mine, wait until there's a break."

"Its okay, I'll miss one game. I'm not even close anyway. Do you want more tea?"

Jean looked worriedly up at Gladys as she stood, strangely, in the middle of a game. Jean had also felt the sadness, but knew where it came from. Her husband and daughter were calling from the other side, from the Spirit World. She wondered if Gladys felt them call. "No she's too young, too caught in this world to hear the dead people talking." Jean went back to the game.

Noise and Confusion

Jimmy was not certain of the date. He packed his furs into bundles. The traps were empty this morning so he pulled them all. It was close enough to Christmas to go home. Seventeenth, eighteenth maybe. He started the Elan single cylinder snow machine on the fourth pull of the starter cord remembering old Don Quenell's words, "If it takes more than three pulls on any motor there is something wrong". Well if there was something other than the machine had not been started since early November, it would have to wait for repair. Jimmy was in a going-to-town mood. First he would sell his fur at Robertson's Trading Post, pay Alex back for the supplies, then go see Gladys.

Tom Roberts is the only employee of the CBC in La Ronge. His office, studio, broadcast centre above Robertson's Trading Post, looks out over La Ronge Avenue, and beyond toward the frozen lake. Tom enjoys his large window especially in the winter. A truck will pull up full of kids and the father will go to the back of the truck. A good season, and he might take two, maybe three bundles of fur into the store behind the scurrying children. If not so good a season, only one bundle. An hour later the children come into view with their hands full of pop bottles and potato chip bags. The father and mother load box after box of groceries, clothes and supplies into the truck, round up the children and drive away.

This afternoon Tom watched Jimmy bring his old snow machine up close to the motel across the street and unload the sleigh. He knew it was Jimmy more by his manner than by his appearance. Jimmy looked like any number of Northerners, in a heavy green parka and felt-lined boots. It was the way Jimmy bent from the waist as he pulled at the ropes on the sleigh that identified him. Most people would crouch. It was the straight way of walking across the street without the wasted effort of any swagger that made Tom sure it was Jimmy before he could see his face. Tom felt his pride in knowing this man who carried four bundles of fur to the trading post, wished he didn't have a radio show to prepare so that he could stop in downstairs and visit, ask about trapping conditions. Is everything prime? How are the ice conditions? Is there slush?

Jimmy received all the news from Alex that Charles had been hospitalized but was home again. Henry had been in last week. Mostly Alex talked as always about fur, prices, weather, and quality. He liked Jimmy's fussy way with fur. Everything cleaner than it needed to be. Everything stretched evenly and dry. Beaver in ovals, Fox brushed to a shine and Martin small and very black put a smile on Alex's face. When the counting and running fingers through the fur was done, when the best price Alex could pay for the fur and maybe even a little more was in Jimmy's hand, Jimmy went to look for Charles. It was Friday the twentieth of December and Jimmy figured that late on a Friday Charles would likely be in the bar.

Jimmy endured the sun as he drove his snow machine a little further along the shore of the lake. He left it in the frozen park on the other side of La Ronge Avenue from the hotel and trotted across the street and the welcome dimness of the bar. His eyes adjusted quickly to the meagre light. Charles wasn't there but Edward was.

"Hey James, how you are bro?"

"I are fine, Eddy, I are fine." Jimmy continued the childhood joke of refusing to speak English in what the teachers had insisted was proper. "When did you get here?"

"'Bout an hour ago. Just got off the plane. Came here to see if Charles was around."

"That's who I'm looking for too. Seems he must be somewhere else."

"He'll show up. May as well wait here instead of running all over town looking for him I figure. What say I buy you a drink?"

Jimmy did not want alcohol. He felt anxious and eager, beyond the anticipation of finding Charles. His body and his mind buzzed with energy; something negative was coming and he was ready for it. Edward ordered two double ryes. Ginger Ale in his as always and water in Jimmy's. Jimmy did not object. He was only half listening to his brother who was flirting with the waitress out of habit. Edward was home in the bar. This was his territory, his floor, his chair, his pool table, his comfort.

"So, what happened to Charles?" Jimmy forced calm to his voice.

"He got fucked up over a woman."

"Is that what he said?"

"No, I haven't talked to him yet. But put it together for yourself. Lorna left, Charles shot himself. What other reason is there?"

"I haven't talked to Charles in a long time either. Probably eight, nine months and then we didn't talk about anything. He was drunk and I left him to his pastime."

Edward was beginning to feel uncomfortable. He misunderstood Jimmy's tone and rigid manner as suggesting that Jimmy wanted to have a deeper conversation about their brother and his attempted suicide. Edward wanted to find Charles, give him shit for his stupidity, smarten him up and have done with it. Find the problem, fix it, and go on. He stood up, walked over to the pool table and placed a Loonie above the coin slot indicating to the players that he was next up and would play the winner. He did not want to play pool in particular — without thinking about his actions, he was avoiding an in depth potentially emotional conversation with Jimmy.

Jimmy sat back in his chair, stretched out his legs, picked up his glass of whiskey and water and looked into the liquid swirl. His rippled reflection drew his mind, pulled at him. Jimmy's fear began to rise and he forced it back. Why would he fear whiskey? There were no answers in the glass so he drank it in one long drink. Not out of thirst but to empty the stupidity from the glass. The whiskey stirred the anticipation in Jimmy's chest then numbed it. Jimmy indicated to the waitress with a wave of the glass that he wanted another. It would require patience to have any sort of conversation with Edward and whiskey was patient. He did not attempt to rationalize his fear of his own reflection.

Despite his throat tightening with each drink, Jimmy continued to pour whiskey and water down his throat in single gulps. He refused to acknowledge the fear that accompanied each drink, the same as he had refused to acknowledge his growing fear of sunlight. The alcohol helped Jimmy to ignore his fears. It did not remove them.

Sobriety

"It's not a sin to drink." Uncle Zach's voice was kind and gentle. The cabin was warm and comfortable. Charles stirred sugar into his tea and enjoyed the old smells; the musk of Beaver pelts and wood smoke and cooking. The ancient wood cook stove emanated more than heat. It seemed to have its own presence in the cabin and reflected gentle goodness off the yellowed log walls.

"You can drink as much as you want and the Creator won't get mad at you. It's your choice. Everything's up to you. Just don't blame the Creator when your mind turns to mush and your liver and kidneys quit on you."

Uncle Zach moved around the cabin as he spoke, putting wood into the stove, sweeping up the pieces of bark that fell on the bare wood floor. Finally he sat across the small table beside the South-facing window and concentrated upon Charles. "The white people have all kinds of sins, us Indians only have a few. The difference is, ours are extreme sins, theirs are everyday sins. I once heard a priest talk about the seven deadly sins. I remember him talking about anger, envy, greed, gluttony, pride, lust and sloth. Those are their sins. The Creator never gave us those sins. He never wrote the law on stones for us to read. Instead he wrote the law on our hearts. Only the strongest will look there for guidance. Everything is your choice, Charlie. You alone have to decide what's best for you. It was your choice to use alcohol and drugs. Nobody forced you. And it's okay. You're not going to hell and you don't have to repent anything to the Creator."

Charles sat and sipped his tea, listened and nodded as Uncle Zach gave advice. He appreciated that his great uncle would take the time to talk earnestly with him, appreciated all of the times the old man had tried to talk to him as a child and as a teenager, appreciated that Uncle Zach had not judged him, had not been critical. Uncle Zach had merely smiled when he accepted the pouch of tobacco from Charles. Smiled a smile that said, "I am happy." His old face lit up. Charles did not know of the years of prayer that had been affirmed when he placed the tobacco in his great uncle's wrinkled arthritic hand. Uncle Zach did not tell Charles he had prayed for him, did not say, "I knew, or I could have told you." Instead he invited Charles in for tea, enquired as to his family and their health and only gave advice when Charles specifically asked.

"You only have to tell the Creator what you are ashamed of and forgive yourself." Uncle Zach continued. "The Creator did not give us an everlasting hell. He did not tell us that we were born in sin. It was the Christians that told us that. Our hell is this world. We do not have a Devil or Satan that is evil. We do not even have good and evil. Everything's from the Creator and it's all good. When something happens to a person we say that person is sick. We don't say that person's evil. My grandparents used to tell me about *Wetiko*. They didn't think he was evil, they thought of *Wetiko* as a sickness that people got."

Charles caught that a story was coming and looked up. Uncle Zach paused, drank a little tea to lubricate his voice, and continued. "It seems that before the coming of the white people here, there was this man who had a dream he had eaten human flesh. Don't worry, its wintertime, its safe to tell *Wetiko* stories now. Well, this man had that dream and he was sure he was going to become a *Wetiko*. *Wetiko* will eat anything, rocks; trees; everything." Uncle Zach's spread his arms, indicated the total expanse of the cabin and beyond. "And if you get bitten by a *Wetiko* you're going to turn into one. I think if you have one of those dreams or if you meet a *Wetiko* you should get yourself to a sweat right away and clean yourself off. But this man didn't do that. Instead he told his family that if he started to act strange that they were supposed to kill him. You see, a *Wetiko* can also be a cannibal. That's what we were most afraid of in the old days; that someone would become a cannibal. That's our greatest sin: cannibalism. It seems we all said that about our enemies. The Dene say it about the Eskimo, the Ojibway say it about the Mohawk. That's how it was.

"Well to get back to my story. One day some people came to this man and said, "You've been staying here by yourself for too long. You should come to the village. We are having a celebration. It's not good for you to be here by yourself so much." At first the man refused but the men insisted. Finally the man went with the other two to the village. On the way, he suddenly stopped and said "If you are going to kill me, you have to shoot me through the heart." The man's brother was hiding beside the trail. But he knew that his brother couldn't see him, so he just kept still. The two men said, "There's no one trying to kill you. Come on. Come to the village and celebrate." The man took a couple more steps and again he stopped and said "If you're going to shoot me, make sure you shoot me through the heart." Again the men said to him. "No one is trying to kill you, come celebrate." The man took a few more steps and his brother stood up and shot him. He shot him through the heart, but it didn't kill him. So the two men beat that man to death with sticks. Afterwards, they went to burn the body. But the heart would not burn. It was frozen solid and kept rolling out of the fire. Those men had to put that heart back onto the fire each time and it took all night for them to burn it."

Uncle Zach stood up, a puzzled look on his face. "I don't know why I told you that story. It just seemed all of a sudden like, that it was important to tell you. You never know about these things. Do you want more tea?" Zach reached for the kettle.

When Zach had settled himself again, a fresh cup of tea, two sugars and a little water to cool it, he continued:

"You have to learn to pay attention to your instincts Charlie. That's how the Grandfathers and Grandmothers on the other side talk to you. Sometimes something will happen and you will just know. You have to learn to have faith in these feelings. One time I was crossing the river just North of here and I saw a shape in the snow. It was only shadow and light but it made a pattern that got my attention. I knew the pattern meant I should stop. But I kept walking another few steps. That feeling I should stop became really strong and I stopped. I used my axe to chop the ice to see how thick it was and the axe went through with one chop. There was only about an inch of ice there. If I'd kept walking and not listened I would likely not be here today. The more you learn to listen, the more you pay attention to everything around you, the more you will develop. That's how they done it in the old days. They paid attention to everything around them all the time. Watching for signs. That's where they developed their understanding from.

"Those old people had understanding that no one today can even imagine. They knew when something or even someone was coming. Lots of times, when I was a kid, we would go visiting and the old people would know we were coming and get ready for us. It was a nice feeling. They knew we were coming and made us feel welcome when we got there. This one old man used to say the Raven came to tell him before I came to visit. I was only a little guy and this old man used to tease me about my relative the Raven."

Stories

"Tell me a story *Nokom*." Bingo had left Gladys with a feeling that she could not describe. She was on edge and sought her Grandmother's comfort. Home seemed empty without Jesse. Gladys and her Grandmother had developed a routine of movement through the house. It consisted of keeping distance, respect and privacy. Neither pried into each other's affairs and neither was totally alone. Just the other's presence was usually enough to keep loneliness away. But, tonight after Bingo, Gladys wanted something more.

"What kind of story?"

"I don't know, how about a *Wesakicak* story, something fun?"

"Well, make some tea then, get me one of those ginger cookies and I'll tell you a story." Storytellers should be honoured. Food and tea were the minimum that should be offered for a story.

Settled into a comfortable chair with Gladys playing the young girl sitting on the floor wrapped in her favourite quilt; *Nokom* Jean began.

"Kayas, my Mother used to tell me about this time a woman came to their camp. My Mother was just a young girl then. She said the men had found this woman in the winter walking by herself. She would not talk, or could not talk. She was weak and pitiful. So the men brought her back to camp not thinking anything was really wrong. The people gave her food and tea to warm her but she would not eat and seemed scared of the water. Whenever a child came close to her she tried to bite her."

41

"That's not a *Wesakicak* story, *Nokom*." Gladys interrupted. "Tell me the one about when he burned his ass on hot rocks."

"No, my girl, this one's about a *Wetiko*. The Storyteller gets to pick the story and this is the story that came to me. The story picks you; you don't pick the story. Well, anyway, my Mother said her Mother held on to her all the time they were in the same tent as that woman. The people saw the woman was a *Wetiko*. She was already on the other side and couldn't be helped. They tied her up so she couldn't harm the children. No one in the camp wanted to be the one who killed her. That's all you can do to a *Wetiko* once they're too far-gone. Once they've been bitten by a *Wetiko* and turned into one, there is nothing that you can do but kill them. No one wanted to do it. She still looked like a human. So they just left her. The people moved away in the middle of winter and left that *Wetiko* in a tent by herself."

"You know what that sounds like to me?" Gladys interrupted. "It sounds like maybe the woman had rabies. She'd be afraid of water, that's why they call rabies hydrophobia, fear of water. And she wanted to bite the children. That's a symptom of rabies too. She wanted to bite. Was she salivating?"

"My Mother never said anything about that." Jean's tone indicated that she did not appreciate interruptions. "Anyway, my Mother said they never went back to that place because the woman turned into a *Wetiko* and lives there by Smoothstone River."

New Life

Henry sat in the Flin Flon Café and wondered about tradition. Lois smiled as she talked about her work as a Native Courtworker. How she had always sought justice. Henry was only half listening. This experience of happiness was powerful medicine. It cleared away all the accumulated sadness.

"Is there something wrong?" Lois asked.

"No, nothing, why?"

"You had a distant look in your eyes. I was wondering where you had gone."

"Nowhere, I am here with you. It's a good place. Actually, I wish we could stay here all afternoon."

"We can't, even though I would like to. We have to get back to court. It's getting close to time to leave." Lois wanted to take Henry's hand but decided against it. Henry was mostly from the white world, though there was lots of Indian still there, underneath somewhere. In the white world it was for the man to move first and Lois did not want to confuse him. It was enough that she had invited him out for lunch. They had originally started to talk about a file, but the conversation had moved, under Lois' gentle guidance to more personal matters.

On the flight back to La Ronge that afternoon, during the quiet as Judge Friesen and the prosecutor talked between themselves and Henry pretended to read over his stack of files, he wondered about the time he was in. Everything was in a state of flux. He felt the energy flow through him. Henry did not believe in horoscopes and astrology. But, something was going on. He had won more than his usual share of arguments today. One year ago he had been sour and bitter. That sorrow had followed him for most of the year. There was something going on. Something was going to happen. Henry just knew. He did not know how he knew. He just knew. Even though he would have preferred to stay with Lois, go back to her house out at Denare Beach, he was eager to get back to La Ronge. Maybe he should check up on Charles tonight. Maybe invite him out for supper, and a visit. Henry let his mind drift around his family. It was comfortable there.

Despite his good intentions, Henry did not phone Charles that evening. Instead he spent the evening on the phone with Lois talking about justice, the lack of justice and his feelings of failure in not being able to make a difference. He was in conflict. He wanted to impress her. But he did not want to alienate her with arrogance. He wanted her to know that he was a man of honour, of dignity and respect. He wanted her to know that he was capable of kindness.

Lois heard the tension in his voice across the telephone lines and microwave transmitters. She lay on the futon in the comfort of her cabin, stretched out on her back with the handset of the phone between her and the pillow. She listened as he talked about justice, and responded to the gist of the conversation. She wanted to tell him that she wanted him beside her. She wanted to tell him that the pillow was soft and comfortable. She wanted to tell him that the cabin was warm and the light of the fireplace flickered gently across the room.

Storm

Tom Roberts was not the only person watching as Jimmy packed his bundles of fur across the street to Robertson's Trading Post. Elmer Fisher and Paul Taylor sat in an unmarked truck. Elmer leaned back in the driver's seat, his form of exhibiting patience — he was the senior officer and even though he knew that it irked his partner, he took every opportunity to show Paul that he was senior and experienced. "See that? Four bundles. No way did he trap those legitimately. My bet is that he used poison."

"He might've. But that's Jimmy Tinker. He's known to be quite the trapper by the locals."

"Bull shit. These Indians don't know anything about trapping, or anything else for that matter. I tell you this Jimmy guy might have people fooled into believing he's some sort of great Indian hunter, but I'll bet dollars to doughnuts that he's used poison to get all that fur."

"Well, when he's gone, we'll just go in and see Alex. If the fur has trap marks he didn't use poison. If there are no trap marks we can pay Mr. Jimmy Tinker a little visit."

Jimmy sat and watched Edward shoot pool. He stretched his long legs under the table and leaned back. Despite half a dozen very quick ryes with water, he didn't feel any affects from the alcohol. The room buzzed as people ordered drinks and carried on loud conversations. The waitress brought another pair of ryes to the table. "So, you did good trapping?" She picked up the empty glasses. Jimmy reached for his wallet but Edward slapped a twenty on her tray before Jimmy could pay for the drinks. "Of course he did." Edward stood leaning on the pool cue with a big happy face type smile. "Didn't you know, all of us Tinkers are good trappers."

Jimmy kept out of the conversation. Let his brother flirt with the waitress. The room was beginning to feel small, too small. Jimmy gulped his drink and waited.

Elmer Fisher, in uniform, with a pistol holstered on his hip, pushed the door of the bar open so hard that it slammed against its stop. He walked quickly through the bar, eyes searching for Jimmy in the dim light. Paul followed a quick step behind. Some of the fur that Jimmy sold to Robertson did not have trap bruises. The two conservation officers had seized the fur to send to the provincial laboratories for testing for strychnine. Now to question Jimmy.

There had been debate in the truck as to whether to enter the bar. Paul had suggested that it might be better to wait. The bar had a reputation, but Elmer had assured him that Indians could not fight. He would show Paul how to handle a drunken Indian and get him to confess to using strychnine at the same time. Just behave professional.

Paul understood professionalism. An arrest was just an arrest after all. It did not matter if it occurred in a bar or alongside a highway. He walked behind his partner, watched his back.

"Jimmy Tinker, will you come outside with us for a moment. We have some questions about the pelts you sold today."

Jimmy did not answer. He completely ignored Elmer. He was not trying to be rude. He could not answer. There was at that moment a huge welling up of raw energy within him. If he opened his mouth the energy would rush out. Jimmy sat motionless and waited for the surge to subside. It did not. It grew. His ears began to ring, and then the roar of his heartbeat drowned out Elmer's next words. Jimmy held on. Held tight to his calm. Tried to ride out the rush, the tide, the storm. Then there was an arm in front of his face. He turned to see where the uniformed arm came from and there was a soft white throat. The storm broke. Jimmy feasted.

Elmer was dead within minutes. His jugular vein severed and spurting and draining. Jimmy was now drunk. Completely drunk on the taste of hot flesh in his mouth. The storm surged and crested. Paul backed away and clawed for his pistol. Jimmy was on him before he could undo the snap on the holster. The storm needed the sound of breaking bones for the feast to be complete. Marrow and juices, flesh and bones and joy and energy. Jimmy did not go for the hand clawing at the holster. He had no fear of pistols, or bullets or even death. Death was his companion, was on his side, was the power in his hands and in his legs and in his chest and in his jaws. Jimmy grabbed the uniform with meat in it in a bear hug, lifted Paul off his feet and bent him backwards until he heard bones crunch, feasted on his face. He dropped him in a bundle on the floor and began to jump on him with both feet slamming down on the flailing, screaming body. He surged with the storm with every crunch and snap of broken bone. As sanity returned, Jimmy continued to jump on the broken Paul, but now it was to punish. Punish Paul for being there, for being a part of the feast. Jimmy began to feel again, feel his humanity push the storm aside. Feel a little control returning.

Edward grabbed hold of Jimmy's coat and pulled him away. "You better get the fuck outta here, bro. Someone's gonna call the cops. Come on now. Get it together and get moving." Edward turned Jimmy and pointed him toward the door. Like everyone else who had witnessed the last minute, Edward was in complete shock. It was only that Jimmy was his brother that had forced him to move. Everyone else merely stood and stared as Jimmy bounded for the door, his waiting snow machine, the forest and anywhere but here.

The Morning After

Charles was met with rumour when he returned to La Ronge.

"Jimmy was drunk in the bar and killed two conservation officers."

"Jimmy knifed one and kicked the other to death."

"Jimmy stabbed him in the throat with a broken bottle."

"Jimmy bit his jugular vein like a vampire."

Charles phoned Henry. He was not in the legal aid office; it was Saturday. Tried him at home, then his cell phone. Henry was in his truck, would meet Charles at the hotel restaurant. They found a quiet corner booth away from the other afternoon coffee drinkers.

"So what the hell happened last night?"

"I'm not sure. Edward phoned me from the police station. Wanted me to tell the police to fuck off for him. He wasn't talking and the police wanted answers. I guess he was with Jimmy when it happened."

"That's what I want to know. *What* happened?"

"From what I have been able to put together this morning, Jimmy and Edward were in the bar looking for you . . . "

"I haven't been in the bar for a better'n month."

Henry raised his hands in a gesture of uncertainty, opened his mouth but no words emerged.

"Never mind. How could they have known, or you for that matter. I've been keeping pretty quiet recently. Maybe I should've gotten hold of you guys earlier."

"Might've helped, but nothing we can do about that now. I'm not sure where Edward went. I've been driving around looking for him all morning. He wasn't at Gloria's. His kids haven't seen him. Not even a phone call that he was in town."

"What about Jimmy?"

"On the run by the sounds of things. The police were at my place this morning looking for him. What I was able to gather, he had his snow machine in front of the hotel with his sleigh. He had just come from the trapline. Maybe he went back there. I talked to Alex Robertson. The conservation officers seized all the fur that Jimmy brought in yesterday. Suspected use of strychnine."

"What the hell. Jimmy wouldn't use poison. Doesn't have to."

"The fur didn't have trap marks on it."

"Them crazy fuckers never heard of dead fall traps. When Jimmy doesn't have enough white man traps he uses dead falls. Says they work better, more humane too."

"The use of poison will have to be proven by the prosecutor. But that is not the problem anymore. Jimmy is facing two counts of first degree murder."

"First degree?"

"I'm certain that prosecution will press for first degree. It was after all conservation officers on duty. They will try to make comparisons with killing an RCMP. Automatic first degree."

"Twenty years?"

"Twenty-five is life, but there is a possibility of judicial review after fifteen."

"Jimmy couldn't handle fifteen days. He'd go nuts."

Cabin

Gladys pushed her car faster than she had ever driven before. Down the paved blacktop, then a left turn onto the gravel highway that led to Creighton. She checked her rear view mirror often to make sure she wasn't followed.

Jimmy was where she knew he would be — at her Grandfather's old cabin on the Nipikimew River, a hundred yards from the highway. She did not speak. Just wrapped her arms around him and held him close. She felt her love pour out of her chest into Jimmy. It was a physical sensation. It felt like fluid draining. She felt it flow and ease the pressure that had been there. She heard herself think, "This is what love feels like."

"Are you okay?" she finally asked.

"I'm not hurt."

"But are you okay?"

"I will be." Jimmy assured her.

"We have to figure out what to do."

"It was my doing Gladys. You're not involved." He pushed her back, held her at arms length and looked into her face.

"Anything that happens to you, happens to me, Jimmy Tinker. I made you a promise that I would always wait for you. I'm going to keep that promise."

"I'm not going to jail if that's what you're thinking." He let her go and walked toward the window.

"Whatever happens, happens." Gladys followed him. "You don't have to make any decisions right this minute. I just want you to know that I'll be right beside you. But I need to know what happened last night. You don't have to tell me right now, but as soon as you are ready, I need to know."

Jimmy stared out the frosted pane of glass at the trees and the snow. Gladys came up and stood beside him, looking at his face. "The police came to the house this morning asking about you. Theresa was in the bar last night; she phoned me right after you left." Gladys paused. Jimmy remained silent. She kept talking to fill in the emptiness. "They wanted to know if you had any weapons with you. I just kept saying I didn't know, that I hadn't seen you since October. They had a dog in the truck"

Law

Staff Sergeant Joseph McQuay looked through the detachment window out toward the lake at the blowing snow. Why the hell did people get so crazy? Leave this Jimmy guy alone for a while and he would undoubtedly show up at the station and turn himself in, as soon as he sobered up and his family had a chance to talk to him. If the environmental brass had their way, Joe would have to mount the biggest manhunt since the mad trapper Albert Johnson. Joe had been a Mountie for twenty-five years; never seen one evil person in all that time. Seen lots of pitiful people, people with problems that had to be removed for the safety of the community but no evil people. The conservation officers and now the media were going to make this bar room fight into some kind of cannibal freak show.

Joe turned away from his window, the best part of his office, and answered the knock on his door.

"I've made enquiries with Ottawa; there is a possibility that we can have access to a satellite to assist in the search." Constable Chris Reid announced.

"A satellite?"

"Yes, sir. Through our anti-terrorist connections with the States. We can have limited access to an American satellite with infrared surveillance."

"Hold off for a few days. I'm sure that the expense will not be appreciated by Headquarters if this trapper walks into the office as soon as he sobers up."

"If I may, sir, I believe that if we do not get on this right away the chances of catching the killer diminish in proportion to the time from the incident."

Right out of the textbook, thought Joe. Too bad there wasn't a northern or real person textbook.

"I am aware of the established practices, Constable. This is not a matter of identification of the accused. We already know that. All we have to do is bring him into custody."

"That is my point, sir. We have to find him to bring him into custody. He has sought to elude us. And there is the fact that he killed a uniformed conservation officer while on duty, sir. I believe that it is imperative that we take him into custody as soon as possible if only to soothe the concerns of the public."

And if people did not go crazy over a bar room fight, they would not create public concern, Joe thought. But he answered the eager officer, "Go and check on his girlfriend again, what's her name? Gladys? He'll show up there at some time or another. Maybe you should get an unmarked car and place her house under surveillance. You can take the day shift."

Joe chuckled to himself at the idea that came to him while he was giving the order. "Let's see this textbook surveillance on a reserve." It would put techno cop out of the office and make him think he was actually doing something. Maybe he would even learn something.

"And the satellite surveillance, sir?"

"When we have a place to start looking for him. You can look a long time in this country, even with a satellite. By the time you have things narrowed down a little, we can talk again about using satellites and other technologies. Until then we will use good old-fashioned police practices. He'll probably come to his girlfriend's place for supplies, I figure." Joe was pleased with himself. It was true that Jimmy would likely show up at his girlfriend's place. Maybe techno cop would even catch him there.

"Yes, sir. I will arrange the surveillance of Gladys Lonechild's house immediately, sir, and I will personally stand the day shift. And for your information, I have made the arrangements for DNA testing of the samples taken from the two officers."

"DNA?"

"Yes, sir. We should find saliva around the wounds."

Joe sat back down and stared out his window again after Constable Reid left. DNA. What the hell was that about? There was no need for DNA testing when there was a room full of witnesses who saw Jimmy bite the officers, and their statements were all consistent. That was the best part of working in the North; very rarely did anyone ever lie. They would avoid telling you anything, but when they did, it was usually the truth.

Joe mentally reviewed what he had while he watched the snow blow across the frozen lake. The conservation officers had sought to question Jimmy based upon an ongoing inquiry into the use of strychnine. Jimmy had just returned from the trapline and was in the bar drinking with his brother Edward. The waitress said that Jimmy had been drinking very hard, drinking doubles as quickly as she could bring them. He had eight or ten before the conservation officers arrived. No one witnessed the first killing. Most people were looking away as the officers approached the table. There had been no sign of trouble at first, just an embarrassment.

Joe understood — the people in the bar had been embarrassed for the conservation officers, the way they marched into the bar, the way they behaved, their obvious arrogance. No one wanted to watch. They had averted their eyes to spare Jimmy the added embarrassment of their stares. But, when Jimmy was stomping the second officer and biting his face, everyone was watching. They saw Edward pull him off and saw him run from the bar.

Jimmy was known in town. He was a local, grew up here. Had a girlfriend to everyone's knowledge, an ongoing thing for several years. But unlike most couples in the North had not taken up residence together. The story was Jimmy was afraid of her grandmother. Both his parents were dead and he had three brothers. Charlie was well known to the police, never for anything criminal, just drunkenness. His brother Henry was a legal aid lawyer and a local success story of sorts. His brother Edward was an unknown. Had lived in town some time ago, married to a local woman Gloria. Worked the mines. A tough nut. He had been brought in for questioning and merely frustrated the officers with his refusal to say anything and his insistence upon his right to remain silent. Edward was still in cells. They could hold him a while longer on drunkenness but would have to release him soon.

Joe was angry. Angry at spending all Saturday in the detachment instead of at home. Angry at the officers for their arrogance in marching into trouble, for looking for trouble. Angry with the people who were turning a routine bar fight into something larger than it was.

Well, maybe it was a little more than a bar fight. Conservation officers killed in the bar was going to cause excitement. And the rumour that Jimmy had bitten the first officer's throat, now that was sensational. It would sell papers and television time. The local radio station was announcing the murder but to its credit had not mentioned the details. None of the witnesses swore that Jimmy had bitten the officer's throat. That was conjecture based upon his having been seen biting the second officer's face and the lack of a weapon. The wounds did look like bite marks. But they might have been knife wounds or some other weapon that he carried out with him. There was no sign of a broken bottle, though.

Now, Joe knew he had to find him before this blew completely out of proportion. The big factor was the Department of Environment people. They were pissed. Dead officers on duty. Here was the proof of their insistence upon being allowed to wear side arms. Joe wished the government had never caved in and allowed them to have guns. What good were side arms when the people they were supposedly dealing with had rifles? Angry conservation officers armed with pistols could only lead to more trouble.

Waiting

Jimmy settled down to wait. He had enough food, shells, and firewood. He had all the time in the world. He tried to think his way out. There was none. Gladys was certain that he had rabies. If that were the problem, he would be dead in a few days. He had read all the bulletins over the years about rabies. He knew the symptoms and the causes. Why the hell had he not thought of it when he was bitten? Rabies had not even crossed his mind. Well, if he had rabies, it would be best to stay away from people. Maybe go out into the winter without his parka, sit under a tree and wait until he felt warm and sleepy. They said once the shivering stopped, freezing to death was the nicest way to go. Didn't the old people used to go out in the winter once they felt they were a burden on their families? Maybe they knew something about the best way to die.

Yet Jimmy was uncertain. Rabies had definite symptoms; the brochures to trappers had said that it took three or four months before it became full blown. He had another month maybe more to go, if he had rabies. It was supposed to cause him to be weak and demented. He felt completely alive and healthy. That is, at this moment he felt completely alive and healthy.

Last night on the way South to the cabin he had not been so coherent. His first clear thought was that the snow machine was running too rich. He had pulled off the carburetor cover while the machine lugged across the frozen lake and reached down with his left hand to adjust the needle valve. Less than a quarter turn tighter and the engine raced. His thought was that the adjustment would preserve fuel. He remembered that the reason he had started to make the adjustment was from a desperate need to travel faster. He had come back from his dream world in that windy moment as he fled the horror of his own making.

Once the panic subsided he'd continued heading South. The cabin on Nipikimew River became his best choice. Here was the place where he and Gladys had spent their first summer. Her Grandfather had built a snug cabin, close to the highway and close to the river, mid point between two worlds; the modern world of cars and trucks and the old one of traps, canoes, and the river system; the original highway.

Jimmy remembered that first summer as he looked around the sixteen by sixteen foot cabin. How many times had they made love here, and outside and along the river and even in the canoe floating on the river current in each other's arms? It had been a summer of passion and patience. Jimmy waited for Gladys to say that she would stay with him in the cabin; not return to La Ronge and her job at the end of her three weeks of vacation. His patience was not rewarded. As the three weeks drew to an end she had become quiet and began to withdraw. The fantasy world of cabin, river, trees, sunlight and passion dissipated as the reality of La Ronge and work and regular pay drew closer.

Then came the endless discussions. How would they stitch their lives together? Jimmy could not live in town all the time. Gladys could not live alone while she waited for him to return. In the end they returned to the *status quo*. Gladys stayed with her Grandmother and Jimmy "visited". Over the years they had developed their way of being together and their way of being apart.

The thought of rabies pulled Jimmy's mind away from the pleasures of the past. Jimmy was always comfortable in the present and rarely drifted to the future or the past. He had no regrets and was not dependent upon hope. He rationalized that if he had rabies that he was going to die. No one who experienced rabies symptoms ever lived more than a few days. But in this moment he was very much alive. If he began to have serious symptoms he would walk out into the trees and take off his parka.

Rabies aside, Jimmy had to find his way through that moment of insanity and the death of two officers. He remembered the *Wetiko* stories. But they were just stories. He would not even allow himself to imagine that answer. His questions were about his mind, his motives, his actions. There simply were no rational explanations for what had happened. He'd have to just let it be. The answers would come in time, and it would just take longer if he tried to force an answer from a mind that had betrayed him.

Watching

Gladys felt sorry for Constable Reid. He looked completely out of place in the government four-door Chevrolet. The car's newness stood out on the reserve more than anything else. Every new car was known, as was every old car. That it was clean made it stand out all the more. Constable Reid slouched his large frame in the driver's seat and tried to be invisible.

Maggie Clark watched him and the car without trying to hide her stare. He was, after all parked in front of her house. At first she had waited for him to come in. Now she stood clearly visible, framed by her large living room window, and stared openly at the rude officer who parked in front of her house as though she had done something wrong. Maggie knew that Constable Reid was watching Gladys. Knew about the killings in the bar on Friday. But that did not give the police the right to park in front of her house. They had no right to bring her into this, to implicate her. Who was going to come and visit her, with a police car parked all day in front of her house?

Constable Reid was fully aware of Maggie's stares. But, he was reluctant to move the car to another spot. From here he could see Gladys' house and any approach. There simply was no other place to park where he could conduct the surveillance. The problem was that there was nowhere that he was not *also* under surveillance. The hardest time was when the school bus let the children out right beside the car. Some of the children came to the car to visit.

"What are you doing here?"

"Are you watching Gladys?"

"Are you going to catch Jimmy Tinker?"

"Do you have a gun?"

"Is Jimmy a *Wetiko*?"

Gladys watched Constable Reid and the car; watched Maggie watch, and watched the lack of people out there. People were staying in their houses. The usual squads of young people wandering between friend's houses had completely ceased. The presence of the car disrupted the normal flows of the reserve. Gladys wished the constable would leave. Quit wasting time here. Jimmy was not coming to visit her. Would never voluntarily return to town or civilization again. The damn fool was going to die out there. Her fears came rushing home and filled her with anxiety that forced her from the window and the slightly parted curtain.

Jimmy was going to die out there. Gladys knew, she just knew. There was no other explanation. Jimmy was not a murderer. He was not an evil or even an angry person. The only explanation was that he had rabies. If the police did not find him soon he would slowly suffer and die alone. Jimmy's most difficult time was to be alone. Gladys felt his loneliness mingled with his desire, how he tried so hard to be with her, to be part of a couple, not to be alone. That would be the hardest for Jimmy, to die alone. And this damn fool cop was sitting out there on the road in his stupid government car. He wasn't doing anything, just sitting there. Why the hell didn't he go find Jimmy — force him to come to town and to the hospital?

Christmas

Henry phoned Lois at home. He had hoped to spend the Christmas break with her. There was still time, after all he did not have to return to work until the first Monday in January. Things might be back to normal before then. But he could not leave until this thing with Jimmy was finished or at least put into order.

"What can you do in La Ronge that you can't do here?" Lois looked around her kitchen, and the baked goods, and candles on the table, and the carefully selected decorations. Christmas was a big deal for her; it came each year with memories of before the dispersion, before the family went to the four directions. Lois did not want to be alone again this Christmas, but she did not want to alienate Henry. She purposely kept any hint of a whine from her voice. "I want you here." She almost whispered into the phone. Then, with determination born from her resistance to self-pity, she stated clearly: "But if you can't come here. Then I'll come there."

"I have not done Christmas in years." Henry warned.

"Well, what do you do on Christmas day?"

"I usually go hunting. Best day of the year. All the conservation officers are in town eating dry turkey. There's no one out there except me and about half a dozen Moose that I've chased every Christmas for the last five years. We have a relationship now. They expect me to come chase them around on Christmas day."

"Have you ever got one?"

"Not yet. Every year I spend the day walking in circles trying to get a shot. The Moose, I'm sure, know I am coming, and just play along. But every year I hope that one of them will have pity on me."

"There's good hunting here, too." Lois looked again around her kitchen. She did not want to pack everything and drive to La Ronge.

"Okay." Henry changed his mind in that moment. "I'll be there tomorrow. Later in the day. Are you interested in hunting? I'd hate to change a tradition that I've only just begun."

"We can go hunting." Lois accepted the middle ground. "But when we get back we eat turkey and I guarantee it will not be dry."

Charles wandered around the Friendship Centre. It was not the Thursday AA meeting, but Charles needed some place to be and the Centre had a welcome feel to it. The Kikinak Friendship Centre in La Ronge is the best run Centre in all of Canada, Charles learned from the secretary. It had been there for more than twenty-five years, offering support to Aboriginal people who found themselves in an urban setting. He had never thought of La Ronge as urban, but in comparison to the traplines and bush life that most family histories included, La Ronge was definitely more urban. The problems faced by people here were the same as the problems faced by Aboriginal people in the cities: dislocation, alienation and domination by a race that considered itself elite in the world.

Charles looked in the director's office through the partly open door.

"Yeah?" Ron Churchill acknowledged his presence and asked what he wanted in one syllable.

"Oh, I was just wondering if you could use a volunteer 'round here?"

"I don't need a volunteer. But I do need someone to supervise our youth program."

Charles stood there not knowing what to say, caught unprepared and uncertain.

"No sense working for nothing when you can get paid." Ron continued. "We need someone here in the evenings mostly. Come on in and sit down. You make me uncomfortable standing in the door. We need someone to supervise things in the evening. Floor hockey or whatever. I can give you a salary. It ain't much." Ron rubbed the top of his head. Ran fingers over the brush cut black grey hair. "But you have no money for programs. So be inventive. Whatever you can do to keep teenagers busy and out of trouble that doesn't cost the centre any money. Want the job?"

Fever

Constable Chris Reid was back on duty the next day, dutifully sitting in the unmarked police car in front of Maggie's house. The reserve had adapted to his presence. The visiting resumed but people selected longer routes between houses. Maggie went out and invited Constable Reid in for coffee. "You can watch Gladys from inside." Constable Reid declined the offer and Maggie stomped back into her house thinking, "Let the asshole sit out there then. See if I care if everyone thinks he's an idiot."

Gladys watched the exchange. "What did that old gossip tell him?" she wondered. Gladys paced the house. Measured steps matched measured thoughts. What right did she have to interfere in Jimmy's choice? It was his life. But, what of her life? What of her life alone, with Jimmy dead, frozen, forever gone? Choice? What of choice? Was Jimmy capable of making a choice? Was his mind working properly? Did she have a duty, an obligation to make choices for him? Now that he was sick, shouldn't she take responsibility to make sure he received treatment?

Jimmy stopped in his tracks. "No, Gladys would never betray me." He spoke aloud to push the thought away with sound. "Can't let myself think like that." But the anxious feeling would not leave. The thought kept returning, becoming more urgent with each occurrence. Gladys was going to tell the police where he was. She was the only one who knew.

Jimmy walked to the highway with a snowshoe to use as a shovel. If he could hide a trap from a Fox or Martin, he could hide the tire tracks of Gladys' car to the cabin. One of those big pines across the road would add to the camouflage. Jimmy found a roll of fishing line that brought back memories of catching beautiful Grayling and their sparkling dance, tails on rippled water as Gladys laughed and cheered. Sounds and sparkles mingled in sunlight and water.

The river was frozen. It was December twenty-fourth. Jimmy brought himself to the moment to avoid the anxiety and the memory. Even if Gladys did not betray him, he should take precautions. Then he realized the date — it was Christmas Eve. His wallet was full of money and he had not bought anything for Gladys. He would gladly give up the thirty-five hundred dollars, give up the fur, give up the work and effort of catching the fur if he could take back the last few days.

Jimmy considered Christmas and its lack of meaning. More important to him was the solstice. These were the shortest days of the year. Daylight was only a few hours. Jimmy was not concerned about how much work he could do in the light of day but rather how long he would have to endure it. How long each day he would be visible, vulnerable.

He opened the draft on the stove to quickly burn up the wood. Less smoke to burn it up than to dowse it with water or snow — the fire was mostly coals now. You never know who might drive by on the highway and see that the cabin was occupied. The last thing Jimmy needed was for someone to drop in for tea or offer to share a Christmas drink.

Henry was not thinking about his brother as he drove along the narrow gravel highway toward Creighton and Lois and Christmas. He was thinking that it would be much faster if he had access to the plane the court party used. The man standing on the side of the road looked familiar in the headlights. Henry stopped.

"I need a favour," Jimmy flatly stated.

"What the hell you doing out here?"

"Waiting for you."

"But, how could you know I was coming?"

"Just knew."

Henry shook his head in obvious bewilderment. Here was the man everyone was looking for standing calmly on the side of the highway waiting for precisely him.

"I need shells." Jimmy shoved a handful of bills through the window. "Twenty-twos and .243s. Leave them under the bridge on the Bow River. Get the heaviest grain of .243s that you can."

"Listen Jimmy, we have to talk. You're in serious trouble."

"I know," Jimmy said, and walked away.

The next vehicle to come down that bit of gravel highway was a plain government car.

Staff Sergeant McQuay had known that La Ronge was going to be an active posting. Knew the North and the people and the systems. But this was out of the ordinary. This was not how he wanted to end his career. This was not coasting into retirement. He looked out his window. There was no help out there and he turned back to the phone and the call he had to make.

"I understand you have the preliminary report, sir." Joe wanted to sound official, sound like he had things under control when he spoke to his superiors. "Yes, sir, two officers in the line of duty . . . "Yes, both appear to have been killed with the same rifle. The forensic team from Saskatoon are on their way up. The area is sealed. From what we have been able to put together, Constables Reid and Potter were investigating a tip that the suspect was hiding in a cabin just off the highway to Creighton about eighty kilometres from La Ronge. It appears that they were ambushed. Both officers were tangled in fish line that had been strung between trees all around the cabin.

Constable Reid's weapon was drawn but unfired and Potter never even unsnapped his . . .

"Yes, we discovered the bodies around midnight last night when the constables did not report in . . .

"No, there was no sign of mutilation . . .

"No, no sign of the suspect. There were fresh snow machine tracks travelling north from that location and we assume that he is on his way back to La Ronge . . .

"Yes, I would say it is much more than a damn shame. I have yet to inform the officers' wives . . .

Henry learned of the killings at the exact same time as Charles and Edward. He had been listening with pleasure to CBC radio and Tom Roberts broadcast of Christmas greetings across the North, enjoying knowing the people named and best wishes sent to. The hourly news, with its skimpy details of the killings, interrupted more than the Christmas greetings. Henry sat in Lois' living room, supper half-finished on the coffee table. More romantic in the living room with the dim lights than to have a meal in the bright of the kitchen. Now any thought of romance was gone.

Lois felt her anger rise. Anger at Jimmy for his thoughtlessness, anger for his disruption of the evening she had planned out in detail many times over the last few days. Then she saw the look in her lover's face, saw the pain and sorrow in his slouch. She picked up the plates and took them to the kitchen. Christmas was over. Now she had work to do: lift this man back up so that he could use the strength that she saw in him.

"Do you want to go to La Ronge tonight or wait until morning?"

"There's nothing I can do tonight or even tomorrow."

"But you want to go home?"

"I'm sorry Lois. I wanted to have a nice Christmas with you."

"You don't do Christmas, remember." Lois teased. A smile wrinkled her smooth cheeks.

Henry smiled back. Felt the weight lift from his chest and reached for her. Lois snuggled in Henry's arms. Henry felt the woman there. Felt the warmth and the softness, the tenderness as she laid her cheek against his shoulder. Strength flowed into Henry, his confidence returned. Everything was going to be alright. He would be okay. He wished that he had a plan. But that could wait. Right now as he stood with his arms wrapped around this wonderful woman, he knew he was where he was supposed to be.

Edward slammed his fist against the steering wheel, skidded the car to a stop. "What the fuck is going on!" he yelled at the night beyond his windshield. The seat belt suddenly felt tighter to his six-year-old son in the passenger seat. He wanted his mom right at this moment. An afternoon with dad had been fun. But this sudden change scared Michael. There is not a lot to do in Prince Albert on Christmas. *Lord of the Rings* had been an excellent movie. The fantasy world of elves and dwarfs and hobbits had been fun, but the fantasy world of Father and son came to a crash end with Edward's fist into the steering wheel. Michael started to cry.

"It's okay, Mikey, I'm not angry at you. I'm just upset about your uncle Jimmy. You remember your uncle Jimmy, right? He's the guy in La Ronge that used to give you piggy back rides."

Michael did not remember, could not remember, could barely remember the man who was trying to comfort him. Edward realized his uselessness as Michael continued to sob. He put the car back in gear and pointed it toward his ex wife's apartment. He felt powerless. He hardly knew the boy beside him, and had no idea how to soothe his hurt, or slow the tears. For the first time in his entire life, Edward missed family.

Charles answered the knock on the door. The little girl from next door almost whispered in shyness. "Your brother wants you to phone him in Prince Albert."

"Did he leave a number?"

"Yeah, my mom has it," and she scurried off through the snow back to her new Barbie doll that she had reluctantly left to deliver the message.

Arlene pointed at the phone when Charles arrived and continued brushing her youngest daughter's hair while they sat together on the couch watching television. Before he left, she would assure Charles that she did not think badly of him or his family, and she was not even certain that it was really Jimmy that killed those people. She had known the Tinker family all her life and they had always been good to her. She did not believe the rumours.

Charles thanked her for her words and the use of her phone. He wondered about the rumours. No one had said anything to him. But of course no one would. The rumours were about him and his family. He could imagine the buzz. He avoided a rise of anger. He simply did not have the strength for it and let it slide. The people had reason to talk. After all, there was not a lot to do winter nights. He went home to wait for Edward. It would be a couple of hours before his brother arrived. Charles hoped that Edward would not bring a Christmas bottle. It would be hard to refuse him tonight.

"*Nosisim.*" Jean stroked Gladys' hair. Held her head in her lap and poured her love into her granddaughter. "It will be alright. Just watch, everything will work out." Gladys' sobs subsided. The old voice brought comfort in the time of her greatest sorrow. She had caused the death of the two officers.

"*Nokom*, they would not have gone there if I had not told them."

"It wasn't you who killed them, *Nosisim*. It was not you. It was Jimmy, and it will be Jimmy who pays for it. You shouldn't suffer for his doing."

"But it's not his fault," Gladys blurted. Then she told her Grandmother about the Fox bite, and how Jimmy probably had rabies that affected his mind, and how she knew, and how she made the police promise that they would take him to a hospital before she told them where he was, and how it had all gone wrong, and how horrible she felt, and how it really was her fault, and Jimmy was going to die alone out there.

Jean put her hands under her granddaughter's head and lifted, pushed Gladys to sit up. Pity was not going to help. This girl needed straight words.

"*Nosisim*, if there is anything that I know in this life, it is that people pay for their sins. That is why I have told you all of my sins, so that you would know, if something bad came along, that you were paying my sin for me. What we do in this life will come back to us and to our children and grandchildren. That is why we have to walk with truth and honesty all the time. My grandparents told me things. They knew things. For a long, long time we could not talk about those things. Now, *Nosisim* I have to tell you, so that you don't make the same mistakes we all did. Those things my grandparents told me about, those *Wetiko* stories. Those were not just stories to scare children to behave. Those old people knew things. They could see things. The church came along and we had to pretend that we were blind to everything except the Bible. Now your generation walks around and you can't see even the simple things." Jean relaxed her hold on Gladys, smoothed her granddaughter's hair with one hand and kept the other under her chin. She could show kindness, but it was still important for Gladys to pay attention.

"*Nosisim*, if Jimmy has rabies because he was bitten by a Fox, or if he was really bitten by a *Wetiko*, it does not matter.

Whatever happened to him was his fault, or else it is because his parents or grandparents did something they were not supposed to. Maybe it was something as simple as telling *Wetiko* stories when it was not winter. Doesn't matter what it was. Somebody did something and Jimmy has to pay the price for that sin. Now Jimmy has sins of his own to pay for, and there is nothing anyone can do to stop that. Nobody can pardon him from those sins. It had nothing to do with you, *Nosisim*. He is not your husband. You never got married by the pipe or even in a church. Your sins will be paid for by you or your children or your grandchildren, not by the man that you fuck once in a while." Jean lifted Gladys head slightly to make sure she was listening.

"Don't take his sins on to yourself. Don't wish for punishment for his sins. You will get what you ask for. You have a long line of Grandmothers behind you. They give you whatever you want. If you keep saying that it's your fault, they will make it your fault because that is what you are asking for."

Search

Sergeant Rodney Thorson's head snapped back. The fish line across the snowmobile trail caught him in the crease between his chin and his lower lip. The nylon line cut to the bone before it snapped. As he tumbled backwards off his machine, he thought that he had been shot in the face. His fear as he followed the tracks left by Jimmy was that he would be ambushed. The trail followed the winding river. Where fast water caused poor ice, the trail cut through the forest. It was on one of these portages that Rodney ran into the fish line.

It took a while for Rodney to overcome his fear of another ambush. For the longest time he rode hunched over for the protection of the windshield. He finally arrived at the southeast shore of Lac La Ronge. It had taken the better part of the day to travel the few miles from the cabin by the highway to the lake. It was not just that Rodney was forced to be cautious of an ambush or a trap. Jimmy's Elan snowmobile was much narrower than the police model. Where Jimmy merely wound through the portages, Rodney was forced to cut trees to widen the trail. Several times during the day he had wished that he had a regular axe or even a chainsaw instead of the nearly useless hatchet.

Jimmy's track headed out onto the bay and rounded Fox Point. Rodney followed closely, driving on top of Jimmy's packed trail as he had done all day. As the trail rounded the point, the track disappeared. The light Elan rode up on top of the wind-packed snow and simply vanished. Rodney took his bearings as daylight faded in the west. He was on the southeast shore of Lac La Ronge. The skis on his snow machine pointed directly across the lake to the town of La Ronge, fifty kilometres to the west and slightly north. Rodney stood on the machine and surveyed the wind-swept lake. There was no doubt in his mind that Jimmy had gone back to town.

While the business owners in La Ronge would all state publicly that they wanted Jimmy Tinker captured as quickly as possible, privately they wished that the search would last. Sixty extra police officers in town filled the hotels and motels. The restaurants were all doing brisk business. Gasoline sales were up and there were purchases of snowmobile parts and repairs. The search for Jimmy Tinker created an economic boom at a time when tourism was slow.

The juvenile crime rate plummeted. Young people stayed in at night. There would be few who admitted that they were afraid of, or even believed in *Wetiko*. But wandering around after dark looking for excitement took on a whole new dimension. Not only was the town swarming with police officers, there was a very real chance in the minds of the youth that they might meet up with Jimmy Tinker.

Staff Sergeant McQuay felt more relief than disappointment. Joe was certain that he was vastly more experienced than the officers now in charge. Maybe he had never directed a search of this magnitude, but he did know about northern people. At the same time he was relieved. Retirement waited in seven months. Years of hard work and overtime had sapped his energy. This new division of authority suited him just fine. The Jimmy Tinker file would be handled by Inspector Rolf Spross and Joe would continue to take care of other local matters. Joe was out and really did not mind. A senior officer in charge would take him out of the spotlight.

The view from his window was blocked by the semi-trailer, now parked beside the detachment. Constable Reid would have loved this, Joe imagined. Satellites and computers and technology — all unobtrusive in a plain white rectangular box on wheels. He would have guessed that there would be all sorts of antennae and wires on the trailer. There were not. The metal-sided trailer stood there, between Joe and his lake, colder, he thought, than the ice of the lake, cold and foreign to the North and the people.

But what did he really know about northern people? In twenty-five years of police work he had never encountered a Jimmy Tinker. Was the man a crazed killer? Or was he like Joe had originally thought — just a trapper caught in circumstance? A helicopter chopped the air, vibrated the detachment, and settled down out of sight behind the trailer. Joe turned away from the window.

Jimmy lifted the cowling on the Elan and checked the fuel tank. It was still half full. There was one jerrycan on the sleigh. He calculated a day and a half of travel if conditions were perfect, no slush or soft snow. But, where was he going? Jimmy returned to the shelter of the large Spruce tree, whose wide swooping branches enclosed a space next to the trunk high enough for him to stand. He struck steel to flint and sparked a fire in the tinder of lichen and shavings. Remembered when he purchased the little package in a sporting goods store, and how he had wondered whether he would ever actually use it. He refolded the modernized ancient device and carefully put it away.

Fire was a risk. Someone might see the smoke or even the heat rising in wavy billows of vapour against the sky on a cold day. Jimmy hoped that the dense branches would dissipate the smoke and vapour. He needed heat. Cold to the core. It was a cold that he could not get rid of, a strange feeling of cold that did not cause him to shiver. It was like his heart was turning to ice. Jimmy kept his fire small, not more than a hatful, and laid beside it, brought his chest close to it, opened his parka to feel the heat.

Jimmy was calm again. Yesterday's agitation and fear had faded while he was on the trail North. He looked over at the Elan and wondered whether it had anything to do with his returns to sanity. The snow machine was over thirty years old and Jimmy knew every piece of it. He had shed blood on many of those pieces from scraped knuckles while he made repairs. It was a good machine for the North, not as fast as the new machines that were capable of nearly 200 kilometres per hour. Its modest seventy-per-hour burned far less fuel, and its lightness kept it afloat in deep powder snow or slush.

Even though, over the years, Jimmy had repaired nearly every part of the Elan, it was for the most part very dependable. Its narrow stance made it easy to tip, but at the same time allowed for much narrower trails than those required by the new fast, spring-and-strut suspended machines with their wide apart skis. The Elan was more like a motorcycle than the newer models in that it steered best by leaning, rather than by turning the skies. Rider and machine had to work together and Jimmy had years of familiarity with it.

The fire burned down and Jimmy added a few sticks from his little pile without getting up. The fear of yesterday was gone. When the two constables arrived, they had driven past the approach to the cabin, almost to the river, before they reversed and turned in on the trackless lane. Jimmy's fear had been in frenzy. It had been building all afternoon. Images of hunters pursued him. Torches and screaming mobs pushed all rationality from his mind until he sat crouched with his .243-calibre, lever action rifle behind a large wind buckled Pine.

He was waiting for his hunters when Constables Reid and Potter stepped out of the car, climbed over the fallen tree and headed toward the dark cabin. Jimmy did not move. He watched through the open sights of the rifle as the two officers continued in file through the carefully swept snow. It was when they tangled in the fish line and began to yell and curse that the fear in Jimmy completely overrode all rationality and he opened fire.

Two quick headshots and Jimmy was fleeing. There was no thought. He had reacted to his fear and nothing more. There was no animosity, no hatred, no loathing. Jimmy added another stick to the fire and tried to think his way through.

The fear began to build again. Seemingly from nowhere, it rose in Jimmy's chest, began to tighten and squeeze. Something was coming. Something scary. He placed a large clump of snow on his tiny fire, zipped his parka and rolled over belly down on top of it. From where he lay, he had a clear view of the lake. He gently took his rifle down from where it leaned against the tree, pulled the butt to his shoulder and laid his cheek to the stock.

Rodney Thorson no longer felt the cut on his chin. The cold stopped the bleeding and he gave it no further thought. His thoughts now were on getting back to La Ronge. His earlier fears of ambush had vanished in the cloud of snow thrown up by the machine he raced across the lake, past the island where Jimmy watched him through the open sights of a rifle.

Charles rolled out of bed at 5:15 AM. This was the best part of sobriety. He had learned to enjoy the early morning coffee and cigarettes and quiet. These hours belonged to Charles, to indulge and absorb. He'd developed the habit of listening to CBC radio, for "the news and weather" he said to himself. But there was more. The radio was a friendly voice. It was company in these early hours.

This morning Charles did not turn on the radio. Edward lay asleep on the couch, unaware of the bullet hole in the cushion, gently snoring. Last night had been nice, Charles remembered. It had been years since he had talked with Edward and even longer since he participated in intelligent conversation. It brought back memories of visits with Henry when Henry was in university. Charles and Edward had talked about generalities, nothing in depth, nothing stressful, but not gossip either. The evening flitted from one topic to the next and then it was after midnight and they both felt the weight of the day pull at their bodies, their minds and their eyelids.

Charles was glad that Edward had not brought a bottle. His brother could be very inconsiderate of others, and despised weakness of any sort. Charles had worried that Edward would arrive insistent upon a drink for old times' sake. Charles was just beginning to enjoy his new sobriety. No hangovers, no memory lapses where he worried about what he might have done. His appetite had returned and he could differentiate between hunger and craving. Not that long ago, alcohol satisfied both and he only ate as an afterthought. Charles decided upon bacon and eggs for breakfast. Edward would enjoy them, he thought, not realizing that Edward ate bacon and eggs every morning in the cafeteria at the mine site.

While Charles busied himself in the kitchen with breakfast and coffee and washing out last night's cups, he felt a deepening sorrow begin to rise. It seemed to come from nowhere. He stood there, completely still for a moment, plastic spatula resting in splattering bacon grease and simply felt the sorrow. He let it pull at the rising lump in his throat and push the first brave tear onto his cheek. This was new, he was crying and feeling and it was not horrible. It was okay. Charles could feel again. The empty spot was healing.

At six o'clock Charles turned on the radio for the news and to wake Edward, then went back into the kitchen to serve breakfast. He barely heard the National news broadcaster and was not paying much attention as he examined his feelings and portioned bacon, eggs and homemade hash browns onto the plates. He did hear Edward's loud "What the fuck?" Charles could not imagine what might have brought the outburst. Maybe one of the many mice that shared the house.

"Did you hear that, Charles?"

"No, what?" Charles came into the living room wiping his hands on the sides of his jeans.

"They're saying Jimmy has rabies."

It was Charles' turn to exclaim, "What the fuck?"

"Have you heard this shit before? What the fuck is this?" Words were not coming and they both stood in silence and listened to the announcer. CBC would have the provincial medical officer on later in the hour for an interview about rabies in humans.

Henry rolled over and looked out the window of the town house. He did not recognize the car parked beside his truck and could not guess who might be knocking on his door. He was careful to tuck the blankets around Lois as he got out of bed. Henry turned up the thermostat on the hallway wall as he headed to the front door. Much easier than making morning fire. The memory of younger days caught his mind and was pushed away with thoughts of Lois, her beauty and her warmth and that he did not want her to wake to a chilled house and whoever was at the door and damn he should not have turned the thermostat so low last night. The house was very cold on his bare legs and feet.

Henry welcomed his two brothers into his home, but not the news they brought. The radio news at 8:00 AM repeated the story and Henry listened, coffee in hand. Charles and Edward sat at his kitchen table, likewise quiet, and listened intently.

"It provides a possible defence." Henry broke the silence just as Lois emerged from the bathroom, dressed and beautiful.

"Lois, meet my brothers, Edward and Charles." Henry's formality brought a glance his way from Edward.

"What defence?" Lois asked.

"If Jimmy has rabies, there may be a defence similar to temporary insanity"

"If Jimmy has rabies, he's going to be dead within a few days." Charles realized where this morning's sorrow came from as he almost whispered the words.

"Jimmy doesn't fuckin' have rabies." Edward's anger surged in defence of his brother. "Sorry for the language." He looked toward Lois. "I was the last person to see Jimmy, and he does not have rabies or anything else the matter with him."

"Then what happened?" Henry demanded, his tone steady and matter of fact.

"Those fuckers came into the bar looking for trouble. Jimmy gave them what they were looking for and a little more. He didn't look or act out of character until they tried to grab him. I think Jimmy just drank too much, too fast."

"Intoxication is another possible defence. Can you say for certain exactly how much Jimmy had to drink?"

"Henry, you're missing the point. If Jimmy has rabies he won't live long enough to make it to court." Charles forced himself back into the conversation, though the sorrow sapped the strength from his voice.

"I am just trying to think ahead. Edward, you were not the last person to see Jimmy. I met him on the road to Creighton on Tuesday about four o'clock. He gave me a little better than three thousand dollars and asked me to buy him ammunition."

"Did you?"

"What did he say?"

"How did he look?"

"Did you see the police?"

The questions came from all directions at once. "He didn't give me a chance to ask questions. He just asked me to buy ammunition, then he walked away."

"He walked away where?" Edward wanted a direct answer to his direct question.

"He walked away into the trees. I didn't follow him. I didn't even get out of the truck. He looked like Jimmy. What can I say?" Henry tried to answer all of the questions.

"Where?" Edward insisted.

"About half-way down the cut across, before the turn off to . . . " Henry paused, then remembered. "It was close to the Nipikimew Bridge, I had just passed the turnoff to the sand cliffs."

"Gladys," Charles said. "Her Grandfather had a cabin out there. I bet Jimmy was hiding there. Now it makes sense where he killed the cops. The radio had it wrong."

"The radio is wrong about lots of stuff. Now they're saying Jimmy has rabies."."Who's Gladys?" Lois cut in.

"Jimmy's steady." Henry told her. "Has anyone talked to her?"

The Watcher

Jimmy felt watched. He kept looking into the tops of the trees for the watcher and found nothing. He passed it off as possibly nothing more than a Squirrel. But rationalization did not make the feeling go away. Someone above him was watching and it was not God. God had not looked at Jimmy in a long time. The feeling seemed to come at regular intervals throughout the night. Now that daylight was appearing, Jimmy decided to snuggle in for the day. He gathered firewood, small dry branches from the underside of nearby Spruce, some birch bark that was handy, and Poplar about the size of his wrists. He broke the wood up and piled it where he could reach it. Then he broke green Spruce boughs for his bed and lay down, comfortable in his nest by the tree trunk.

He tried to rationalize his situation, once the fear of being watched had passed. Jimmy knew that he did not have rabies. That diagnosis was definitely out. But what then brought on these fears and anxieties that led to disaster? The *Wetiko* stories came rushing back. Jimmy ran them through his mind and dismissed them. He could not accept them as anything more than his Mother's attempt to make him behave.

Jimmy added a single piece of Poplar to his fire. It would burn without much smoke and last longer than the Spruce that snapped and crackled and quickly burned away. He thought about his Mother as he lay back on his Spruce bough bed. How many years was it since she died? Seventeen, eighteen. He was fourteen at the funeral. The last time his family had been together.

Incredible that they let his Father out of jail for the funeral. But then it wasn't murder was it? He had simply beaten her up one too many times and she died. Five years for manslaughter and his sons sent to foster homes. The four kings scattered to the four directions. Marj Tinker named her sons after kings so that they would have something to be proud of and insisted that each son learn about the king he was named after. Jimmy learned enough to hate King James. He took no pride in being named after a religious bigot. After three years in a Christian foster home, Jimmy never went into a church again.

When he returned to La Ronge upon turning eighteen and was no longer a ward of the Province, he discovered that he was an outcast. He could join the drinking clubs. They welcomed anyone with money. They would even lend money or alcohol until a member found the resources to contribute. Charles joined the clubs. Jimmy could not. The memories they brought back of his Father were too strong.

Was that it? Was he harbouring some deep hatred for his Father that was emerging in insanity? No, that wasn't it. Jimmy pitied his Father. He did not hate him. The man had succumbed to alcoholism. But during his short periods of sobriety, when he was trying to dodge his drinking club, he had taught Jimmy how to trap. Those were the times Jimmy remembered. Walking the trapline behind his Father. The drinking and fighting, screaming and yelling were just background noises in Jimmy's memory of his youth. When Jimmy had managed to trap a Wolf, his Father had bragged him up. Told everyone about his son the great trapper, caught a Mahigan and was only twelve years old.

Then did he blame himself for his Mother's death? The night of the final beating Jimmy had locked himself in the bedroom with his younger brothers and let his parents fight. When they became quiet, Jimmy guessed they had passed out and he went to sleep. His brothers, as accustomed to the fighting as he was and feeling protected by their big brother, had fallen asleep before him.

The next morning, as Jimmy helped his brothers get ready for school, he assumed that his Mother had passed out on the living room floor. Jimmy had stepped over her, even though he knew that stepping over someone was the rudest of all possible actions for an Indian. He had done it purposely in his disgust at her behaviour. He was not aware of his Mother's death until a police officer showed up at the school with questions about the whereabouts of his Father.

If he harboured guilt, it would have shown up long ago. Jimmy put that thought aside. There was nothing about the night his Mother died that was different from hundreds of other nights. Drinking and fighting had been normal. Jimmy did not accept the blame for his parents. He had worked all this stuff through years ago. Trapping allows a person time to think and put thoughts into order. Life on the trapline quickly simplifies things.

Jimmy could not blame his upbringing for his recent actions. Or rather, he would not. He was responsible. Whatever was going on, Jimmy would have to work it out. But it would have to wait. He felt he was being watched again.

Sergeant Rodney Thorson counted slowly to twenty-seven, then released the button on the coffee grinder, poured the fine grind into a French press and waited for the electric kettle to boil and whistle. La Ronge was a nice place. Scenic. But it desperately needed a good coffee house. Rodney preferred dark roast and strong, lightly sweetened. He poured the first cup for himself and the remainder of the press into a high quality thermos bottle. Good coffee should be hot.

He looked forward to his day. Imagine being paid to snowmobile on Lac La Ronge. Stop the occasional snowmobiler and visit. Good coffee, nice weather, nice country. He double-checked his gear before he left the motel. All the mandatory safety equipment in a durable pack; he added his thermos, an extra package of cigarettes and a pair of wool socks. Rodney and a dozen other officers would meet around noon at the hotel for lunch and compare notes. The day would be spent in coordination with the satellite guys in the trailer. Every person outside of town, walking, snowmobiling, snowshoeing or cross-country skiing would be spotted by satellite infrared detection and an officer on a snow mobile would be dispatched to check identity and destination.

The officers were advised to make outdoor experiences uncomfortable. The search for Jimmy Tinker could be best conducted with few people in the area. Infra red detection could identify body heat or a snow machine engine but could not identify a particular person. Rodney pitied the officers responsible for patrolling the town and adjacent reserves. Driving around La Ronge became boring awfully fast.

The search area at present was adjacent to the town, spreading in widening circles outwards. Rodney's partner, Corporal Leon McKercher signalled with a cup to the lips motion that he was going into town for a coffee break, a distance of only a few miles. Rodney waved him on. He wanted to stay out on the lake and have a quiet coffee from his thermos.

Jimmy realized that he had not thought a thought. His internal dialogue stopped some time during the morning. He was thinking about his Father and the words came to an end. It wasn't the uncomfortable silence, like when a conversation abruptly stops. The end of Jimmy's internal dialogue was more like the silence between friends who are comfortable with each other and can accept the simple pleasure of human companionship without having to talk.

Without internal dialogue, Jimmy was in a constant Now. He did not measure one moment against another. He was aware of time, or rather, he was aware of the movement of the sun across the morning sky. But he experienced it as a constant state of Now. He was aware of every sound, every whisper of wind, every bird wing and Squirrel claw on dry Spruce bark.

It might have been the noise of animal activity that brought Jimmy back from that quiet space. All he knew was that urgency was rising up in him. It was not the urgency he had experienced before each episode of disaster. Nor was it associated with his awareness of the watcher. This need to move was related to the activity of the animals around him. The wind was from the East and had been picking up all morning. There was a storm coming. The restlessness of the animals told Jimmy that the storm would last several days. Now was the time to get ready, it was time to eat.

Squirrels and birds are edible, but Jimmy found himself wanting something more substantial. There were snares and traps in the sleigh. He could leave the island for the mainland and trap a Beaver. Turtle Creek was not far; there was a Beaver lodge where the creek ran into the lake. Jimmy did not like the idea. Turtle creek flowed out of a large muskeg and the area was wide open. There would be no place to hide if the watcher came again. But Turtle Creek was on the way to the Bow River. Maybe Henry would bring ammunition. Jimmy felt a need to see his siblings. The feeling moved aside and the need to feed took control.

The smell of coffee stopped Jimmy. He slowly turned his head and sniffed, short quick sniffs so that he could smell with just the tip of his nose. Not deep inhalations that distorted. As his head followed his nose so did his eyes until he could see the dark blue snow machine parked out on the ice. Jimmy's last rational thought followed his amazement at being able to smell coffee from more than a mile away. He thought, where there is coffee, there is usually food.

Renewal

Corporal McKercher slid his hands under Rodney to assist him into a sitting position on the hospital bed.

"Thanks, Leon"

"It's nothing."

"Not for helping me sit up. For getting me to the hospital so fast."

Leon shrugged

"I mean it." Rodney continued. "If it weren't for you, I wouldn't be here. Not that here is such a good place at the moment."

"What happened?"

"Taking my statement?" Rodney forced a smile.

"That too. I want to know what happened to my partner."

"I was sitting on the snowmobile. I had just turned to face out of the wind. I remember those minutes like they were branded into my brain. I mean I remember everything, every detail, the feel of the snow, the taste of the coffee, how many drags I took off the cigarette, everything. I had just taken a drink of coffee and a drag when I felt the bullet hit my head. It must have hit the badge on the front of my hat."

"It did."

"That's what I figured. Then I heard the rifle shot and remember thinking that you were not supposed to hear the one that killed you. My body went slack. I had no control but I was conscious the whole time. I slowly slid off the machine. The cigarette was still in my hand and most of the coffee spilled. The cup was still in my hand when he got there. I can still see him take the cup and sniff it before he drank it."

"Can you tell me what he looked like?"

"What I remember was he looked like he didn't have a care in the world, no reason to hurry. I looked him right in the face when he was standing over me with the axe."

"Holy fuck," Leon exhaled.

"Yeah, I looked right into his eyes. Those weren't human eyes; they were animal eyes. No emotion whatsoever. I can see him clearly, I can see the stubble on his face, and I can see how calm he was. There was no anger. He did not hate me. I was just nothing to him. He stood directly over me, straddled me, and then he chopped off my arm. I remember thinking he must be awfully strong to chop off my arm with two chops with that dull hatchet."

"He used your axe?"

"Yeah, my axe. He took the cigarette out of my hand and took a drag before he threw my arm into his sleigh. He was coming back for the other arm when all of a sudden he looked up. Then he was gone."

"What do you mean, he looked up?"

"He looked up at the sky. I remember wondering if he could see the satellite."

"He didn't look up because I was coming?"

"No, he looked at the sky like he was afraid. You didn't get there until after he left. I remember listening to the sound of his snowmobile getting fainter. I swear I can remember every putt putt of that engine. Then I just laid there wondering how long it would take to bleed to death, when I heard your machine coming."

"You were conscious?"

"All the way to the hospital. I didn't know you prayed. It helped."

"We'll catch him Rod, don't worry — we'll catch the bastard."

"When you find a dog with Rabies, remember to kill it before it can bite someone else."

Food for Thought

Gladys knelt at the front of the church and waited for her turn to receive communion. She thought about the rail in front of her. Why was there a fence around the priest's area of the church? Was it there to confine him or to keep the masses out? The wafer dried Gladys' tongue upon contact. The flesh of Christ washed down with the blood of Christ. Gladys rose from her kneeling position at the rail and slowly walked back to her place near the back of the church.

The red and white Anglican Church on the rock overlooking Lac La Ronge was full this cold Sunday morning. Reverend MacArthur decided on his way to the pulpit to change his sermon from the one he had planned. The church was full because the people were afraid of a *Wetiko*. Today would be the best day to get the message across about paganism. He was concerned about the growing number of sweat lodges in the area. Some were quite visible as he drove around the reserves. The pagan worshippers were becoming bold. It was not that long ago that he could have been certain that heathenism had been totally eradicated. Now it was back and growing.

Reverend MacArthur swished his robes to straighten them as he climbed the two steps to the pulpit. His sermon made it clear that if the people had not abandoned Christ, this evil would not have been visited upon them. He spoke at length on the True Religion, the one religion that was for everyone on the Earth. He reminded the believers that they were part of the mission to bring the word of God to the entire world. Now that they had heard the word of God they could not return to the old beliefs. They could not worship trees and rocks anymore. They could not go back to the time when everyone was afraid, when evil walked the earth. Christ had given his life for them and to return to the darkness would be to turn their backs upon Christ. He was concerned about the small number of people who took Holy Communion that morning. Didn't they know that the Body of Christ and the Blood of Christ was food for their soul? That Christ had given them his flesh to eat?

Gladys sat with her head lowered. She could feel the shame of the people around her, shame for being Indian and stupid enough to have believed in evil things. But Reverend MacArthur was not about to stop at shaming the flock. He went on to make it absolutely clear that if the people did not return to Christ, the old evil would walk the Earth bolder than before and that the true name of the evil was Satan.

Gladys kept her head down. She chose to attend church this morning in search of redemption. The sermon was not redeeming. It only brought more shame and she felt worse than before. Grandmother Jean had refused to come. The old woman had been strangely quiet the last few days since her talk. It was not out of the ordinary for Jean to smudge the house occasionally with Sweetgrass, but now she did it on a daily basis.

Gladys chose to walk after church. The weather was cold and stormy, with a strong West wind that drove snow that felt like gravel into her face. Wind, she remembered, could blow sadness away, could blow bad thoughts away. She tried to give her thoughts to the wind to drive them away but could not and gave up. She walked, face down in the wind, watched her boots move one quick step at a time.

La Ronge Avenue, the main thoroughfare that follows the shore of the lake, is the heart of the town. Businesses had developed and stabilized on either side. Gladys could remember before the pavement and sidewalks, a time of youth, young girls giggling and teasing and daring each other. She wished for that simpler time, and summer and Jimmy. She stopped, turned around and walked back to her car still parked at the church. Jimmy was gone. Somewhere over the last week, or maybe it was the last month, or maybe even longer, she knew that he had slipped away from her. She could not feel his presence inside of her anymore. Those feelings that made her feel so good, so loved and cherished were simply gone and she wondered now whether they had ever been real. Had she really been able to sense when he was coming home? Did she really know when he was hurt or when he was okay? If those perceptions had been real, they were gone now. Jimmy was gone and Gladys felt her loneliness pile up and weigh her down.

Before she opened the door to her car and entered its shelter from the wind she tried once again to reach out and find Jimmy. One more time she closed her eyes and thought about her heart, her core, found the place within herself and willed it to open to the wind. She let her innermost feeling pour and drain away into the gust that grabbed at the fur around the hood of her parka. "All my love Jimmy, all my love. All I am and all I have, *Kakiki mina Kakiki*, forever and ever," she whispered before she drove home to the comfort of Jean, the only person left who cared about her.

Bring It On Home

"Thanks for bringing me with you." Lois cast words into the silence that lay heavy between her and Henry. The radio station from La Ronge had faded out minutes before and Henry had shut it off rather than listening to CBC, the only other station available.

"I'm sorry about everything that happened. I know Christmas is important to you."

"We had Christmas. Anyway, it's supposed to be about family. I really like your brothers. Especially Charles. He has charm about him."

"Charles is charming?" Henry had never thought of his brother that way. Usually Henry was embarrassed and ashamed of Charles. The idea that he might be more than an alcoholic was a surprise.

"In his own way. He's very polite and gentlemanly. And, he is very proud of you."

"What makes you say that?"

"What? That he's proud of you? It's just the way he treats you. Did you notice he didn't interrupt while you were talking? Not at all like Edward."

"No, I never noticed."

"I don't want to interfere, but I think your family has to pull together now."

"What do you mean?"

"It's just a feeling I have. You and your brothers have a distance between you. I think that's what Edward and Charles were trying to do when they came to visit, pull your family back together."

Henry drove in silence. He turned off the pavement onto the gravel highway toward Creighton, still thinking about Lois' last words. The headlights of the truck pushed against the darkness to reveal a narrow band of brown between two snow banks. Traffic on this stretch of road is rare and the darkness resisted the intrusion. Heavy ply tires rumbled on the gravel and vibrated the cab. The darkness swallowed the sound and the silence felt as thick as the night.

"Are you going to leave him the ammunition?" Lois asked as they approached Bow River.

"Don't know."

"It must be hard for you. He's your brother. They say blood's stronger than anything."

"I've known Jimmy all my life. He's the big brother that looked out for me. Hell, he even fought for me. Sometimes he took beatings that should have been mine. These things they say he's done, I can't bring myself to believe them. That's not Jimmy. He's not like that."

"I understand." Lois reached over, took Henry's hand off the steering wheel and held it. "I understand. I understand about family and looking after each other. If you want to stop and put that box back there under the bridge, you can be sure I won't tell anyone. Before everything else, I understand he's your brother."

"I have things to think about first."

"Talk to me." Lois squeezed Henry's hand. The pressure pulled Henry's eyes from the road. "No matter what happens, keep talking to me. I sometimes feel you closing up, putting up your walls."

Henry returned the pressure, reassurance that he was there, and not off in the darkness.

"Career choices."

"You have to explain."

"If I'm caught in a criminal act, let's say, aiding and abetting, I could be expelled from the Law Society."

"What's more important to you?" She tugged at his hand and drew his eyes toward her again. "It's your choice. Look at Edward. He went back to work on Friday. What was important to him was his job. No one criticized him for that. You and Charles understood, even I understand, money is important to Edward — "

"With Edward, it's not all about money," Henry interrupted. "He's a workaholic. That mine's as much his home as anywhere is."

"See, you guys understand each other. Your brothers will understand if you choose to risk your standing in the Law Society."

"But will the Law Society understand?"

"Doesn't matter. They're not family."

Henry placed the cardboard box under the bridge. It contained every .243-calibre cartridge available in La Ronge and a thousand rounds of .22-calibre shells. Not that La Ronge had very many boxes of .243s. They are not a common cartridge. The case of .22 shells, twenty little boxes of fifty rounds, were a bargain at the True Value. "Enough ammunition to fight a war," Henry thought as he stepped back from the box.

"If you see Gladys, tell her that I heard her calling me this morning." The voice came from over head. Henry looked up to see Jimmy crouched between the timbers of the bridge, where the riverbank met the structure.

"Okay." Henry had no other words. He took another half-step back and stopped.

Jimmy slid down the bank and stood in front of his brother. In the darkness under the bridge, he appeared to melt into the shadow. The scant light showed a tired, cold face. The face did not match the memory Henry had of his brother.

"Thanks, Henry. This means a lot to me. I can't explain to you what's going on because I don't understand it myself." The voice, at least, was still familiar.

"When you figure it out let me know."

"You'll be one of the first bro. Now you better get going. You don't want to get caught with me."

I Spy

Inspector Rolf Spross was not going to turn over the search to the army. This was his. The Princess Patricia Canadian Light Infantry might have the manpower and equipment, but this was his search, his file. Those bastards in Ottawa were trying to cut him loose. Well, fuck them. Spross had worked hard to obtain this assignment, called in all the favours. He had manoeuvred through the politics and preferences of headquarters. He was not going to sit back and let the army take over. Command might have relented to public pressure or rather pressure from politicians. But Inspector Rolf Spross was in charge of this assignment.

The fuckin' media had turned on him too. What was this bullshit now about not having personnel trained for remote northern operations? This was the RCMP, for christsakes. We are the ones that opened up this useless country. Didn't those reporters remember RCMP on dog sleds! Shit, the RCMP history predates the army, and definitely predates it in the North. The RCMP have more remote northern experience than any other organization in the world. And now Rolf Spross had to let the PPCLI in on his assignment. Well, they could come, but they were not going to be there when the RCMP caught this rabid bastard.

Spross strategized his interaction with the army. He would, of course, be polite, even appear to welcome them. But he would not surrender any of his authority. He would welcome any technological assistance the army might have. He would even keep their ground forces busy in a show of strength within the town. But he would not share more than minimal intelligence information. Knowing the target would remain his strength. He held those cards. He had the reports and statements about this guy and he had the last track on him.

The recorded satellite surveillance indicated that Jimmy Tinker headed south after his attack on Sergeant Thorson. His path was a straight line until the weather front covered the area and surveillance was lost. That would be the territory where Spross would concentrate his forces. The army could patrol the roads and the town where they would be visible and reassure the public.

He paced the narrow space between equipment banks. The trailer parked beside the detachment looked like any other trailer from the outside. It appeared to be just a plain white forty-eight-foot reefer, no different than the thousands that rolled behind semis on any highway. A short set of wooden stairs led up to a door at the middle of the rectangular aluminum-sided box on wheels. Only the path packed in the snow to the stairs indicated that it was not totally abandoned. The antenna built into the roof was not visible from ground level.

Together

Driving back home alone, Henry thought about Lois' words. The headlights of the truck pushed ahead between snow banks and parallel black walls of trees that flanked the highway. How was he going to pull his family together? They had been ripped apart by the department of social services. Each of the four brothers went to different foster homes. Henry's first foster home was in Regina. He remembered the people he lived with as well intentioned, but there was a constant feeling that he was only an additional source of income for a family caught in poverty.

The second, third and fourth foster homes were better off. But problems developed more quickly in homes where Henry was not accustomed to wealth. Issues of property seemed to develop faster in these homes. Henry, accustomed to owning nothing, did not have a developed sense of yours and mine. The bicycle at home had been there for whoever was riding it at the moment. In the second foster home, each child's bicycle was private and exclusive and was not to be even touched, let alone "borrowed", without permission.

Hired

Ice chips shattered by the chisel scattered across the snow. Dan rapidly finished clearing the hole in the ice, reached into the water with a Willow hook to catch the anchor line and began the process of pulling the fish net out from under the ice.

Six Malamute-cross dogs curled in the snow, still harnessed to the oak toboggan, watched Dan work his magic. He pulled the net, carefully, and laid it out so that it would slide easily back under the ice. As the net came out, it dragged with it the occasional fish to flop in the cold air momentarily, then stiffen in the cold. Dan separated the species as he untangled them from the net mesh: Mullet and Burbot for the dogs in one plastic tub, Walleye and Whitefish in the other tub for himself. As he untangled a particularly large Whitefish and flipped the net so that the fish came out tail first, he remembered his Grandfather: *"Find where he went in,* Nosisim. *Don't be breaking the net trying to pull a Jumbo through head first."*

Dan's Grandfather, Roderick, had been very meticulous about fish, with a powerful preference for Jumbo Whitefish. The old man had also been careful about his nets and equipment. Everything had to be in perfect order. His ice chisel could never be dull. Dan remembered the old man running his thumb across the edge each time before he put it to the ice. Nets had to be packed carefully when put away. Hooks for pulling the net mesh off of fish had to be accounted for and never left on the ice where they might tangle in the net.

Dan had inherited that sense of order. It was a trait that skipped his Father, Daniel. Dan was the product of these two men. He not only had their names — he was Daniel Roderick Settee — he had his Grandfather's perfectionist methods of work and his Father's sense of humour.

Dan gave the net a final flip and the eight-pound fish fell to the ice. Flopped once and stiffened. "This one is for Mary," Dan thought as he placed the fish in the tub. He stood straight then and looked around.

This was the same spot where Dan learned to fish fifty years ago, stumbling behind his Father and Grandfather. Old Roderick had lived just over there at that point to the Southeast where the tall stand of Pine cast its shadow onto the ice of the lake. Nothing there now, all overgrown, just mounds to mark where the walls of the house had stood.

Dan saw the ears of the lead dog stand up. He waited motionless for the dog to indicate its reason for alertness, when the cellular phone in his pocket rang.

"*Moshum*, there are some people here to see you." Young Mark spoke with the calm assumed manliness he used only when speaking to his Grandfather.

"What kind of people?"

"Government people."

"What do they want?"

"To talk to you."

Dan looked around, annoyed at the disturbance, made some mental calculations about pulling the net back under the ice, trail conditions and his own lack of concern about government people.

"I'll be home in about an hour and a half. If they want to talk to me sooner, tell them they need a helicopter." Dan enjoyed the thought of his grandson telling government people off. Give the boy some character and independence.

Dan had not finished resetting his net when the helicopter landed. His grandson was the first person out, followed by two men dressed typically like government people, like they never worked in the clothes they wore.

"Can I run the dogs home, *Moshum*? I know the way."

"Go ahead. Just remember they know more than you."

The government people were plain clothes RCMP. They wanted to hire Dan as a tracker, heard about his work in search and rescue, how he figured out that the last missing boy was actually murdered by his stepfather to cash in on an insurance policy.

"Five hundred dollars a day," Dan bluntly interrupted the buttering up.

"That's pretty steep, Mr. Settee."

"That's my fee to catch your *Wetiko*."

"We never said who you were to track."

"I listen to the radio. Jimmy Tinker is the only thing on these days. It couldn't be a lost person. All the real dumb people who get lost are safely in their warm central heated bungalows this time of year. You want my help, it's five hundred a day."

Mary folded Dan's wool long johns and placed them in the open packsack on the bed. "Don't forget your good thermos. You know you love coffee more than you love me."

"You love coffee too, Mary." Dan dodged the intent of Mary's statement.

"Daniel Roderick Settee, you know damn well that I have never drank coffee even once in my entire life."

"Oh yes you have. I know the reason you put your tongue in my mouth is just to taste my coffee breath. I bet you've drank hundreds of cups that way."

"No. I always spit it out on your cock, trying to put some colour back on you."

Dan hated being compared with Caucasians. He was Indian and proud of it. It was not his fault that his Grandfather married a white woman. But this was Mary, his wife. She could tease him about anything, and did.

Mary smiled to herself as she cozied into Dan's arms. Thirty-five years and she had never once let him have the last word on anything. "Where are you going, my Husband?" She deliberately sounded like a very poor actress. This was their rote conversation conducted before each departure of more than a day.

"I am going to get you . . . " Dan paused. He had not thought this part through ahead of time. "A sewing machine, my Wife," he improvised.

"I have a sewing machine, my Husband." Mary was surprised. The usual answer was a new dress or new shoes.

"It's ten years old, my Wife, and almost wore out. You've sewn clothes for me and twelve grandchildren. You need a new one. One of those kind that has its own stand so that you don't have to use the kitchen table."

"My Husband, you be careful. There are dangers on the road."

"I will be careful, my Wife."

"My Husband, don't be looking at other women."

"I will keep my eyes on the ground, my Wife."

Dan wished the RCMP had not agreed to the exorbitant rate he demanded. He had secretly hoped that they would say no, and then he could hold his head up. It would not be that he had refused to help, but that they would not meet his price. But they had met his fee without negotiation. Now Dan was caught by his own words, and Dan's word was his most important possession.

"Here, *Moshum.*" Dan's grandson handed him the thermos Grandmother had sent him to find. In the other hand he offered Dan's seven-millimetre Browning semi-automatic pistol.

"Do you think I'll need this?" Dan looked carefully at his grandson. Was this boyish whim or was the boy exhibiting the intuition that Dan was learning to trust?

"I think you should take it, *Moshum*."

Driven

Jean pushed the smoldering braid of Sweetgrass into each corner of Gladys' room, under the bed, lifted her pillow and let the smoke drift up and cover it. "So that she isn't troubled in her sleep." Jean continued on to smudge the entire house, to drive away the dark thoughts, the negative that clings to people and things. She thought about St. Patrick driving the snakes out of Ireland with a staff. Knew the mythical snakes were the Druids, Earth worshippers like her. Oh, she would love to meet St. Patrick while she held a braid of Sweetgrass. Who would drive whom?

Jean had enough of this *Wetiko* talk, of people's fears, of running off to church; enough of her granddaughter crying in the night, not eating, not laughing. It was time to fix things. That damn Jimmy Tinker was the cause of this. In the old days a man could not talk to his mother-in-law and she could not speak to him or about him. That single, simple rule kept trouble out of the camps. But Jean was not Jimmy's mother-in-law. Sure she acted like she was, but Jean was Gladys' Grandmother, not her Mother. Grandparents have privilege, the right to speak. Even if Jean could not find Jimmy to tell him her mind she could talk to his brothers. That was a more proper way. If those boys would not listen and do their duty she would have to talk to their great uncle, Zach. No, Jean mentally reversed, Zach would be where she started. Grandparent to Grandparent.

Jimmy felt the pull of loneliness and immediately pushed the thought away. He could not afford those thoughts. Everything

Jimmy wished for he got, along with the consequences. He had to be extremely careful with his thoughts — wish for something and he might slip back into insanity and go get it.

Jimmy no longer thought that he might have a mental or emotional illness. But, he knew what it felt like to lose his soul. He knew what it felt like not to be human. He did not have two personalities. He was fully aware of his actions when he slipped. He fully participated in those actions. There was no other to blame. He was not possessed. When he frenzied he was not out of control. Hunger was fed. Safety assured. The only real difference between the two states of consciousness was that his only concern when he frenzied was the immediate. The moment became magnified until the moment became all that there was. He did not lose the concept of consequence. He calculated every action in extremely rapid detail and acted according to those calculations. The reason he feared slipping back into that state was that when he was there, his soul was somewhere else.

Jimmy could not allow himself to feel loneliness. Not even here in the dark of the Beaver lodge where he hid from the Watcher. If he allowed himself to feel the need for company, his soul would leave and he would go find people. People were a danger to Jimmy. His only safety was isolation. More importantly, he knew that he was a danger to people. This realization and this realization alone separated the two states of his being. During frenzy it did not matter what happened to others. All that mattered in the magnified moment was for him to satisfy whatever urge, desire or want he experienced. The frenzy was Jimmy expanded to fill the void of the moment.

Jimmy found he could control the frenzy by controlling his discomfort. He accepted the cold and hunger as just the way things were. If he wanted to be warmer he had only to light the rag. The heat of his makeshift stove, a rag in a tiny can of grease, easily heated the interior of the lodge. Jimmy assured himself again that he was safe and warm.

The lodge was four feet thick, made of mud and interwoven sticks. Even a Bear would think twice about trying to dig him out. The entrance opened above the ice thanks to a worker from the Department of Highways who broke open the Beaver's dam too late last fall for the Beaver to repair before freeze up.

Jimmy's trail to the culvert under the highway was hidden by Willow for most of its length. Where it was open he was careful to cover his tracks with new snow.

Most of the last Beaver to inhabit this lodge remained cut up and wrapped in its own pelt to keep it from freezing. Jimmy had enough food to last. His only problem was time. Time dragged at his mind, time tormented him. During a frenzy, time was Jimmy's friend. He experienced everything as though people and things moved in slow motion and only he moved at a normal speed. In frenzy, time did not exist. Everything fit into a single giant moment, with Jimmy at its vortex. When his soul returned, time came back to torture him.

Jimmy's hand reached out and snatched the rifle. A slight vibration in the ground indicted that a car was approaching. He sat motionless and listened intently as the volume of the sound increased, reached its apex when the car passed the lodge and began to diminish. Jimmy memorized the sequence of sounds; any variation might indicate danger.

When silence returned, Jimmy sat in the lodge with his deepened sorrow. How could he return to the people if the sound of a passing car caused his soul to flee? His feet felt cold. Jimmy needed better boots.

Glimpses of Nothing

Constable Clifford Rhode intently faced the large computer screen. His work area occupied one end of the trailer and consisted of a bare desk, keyboard and monitor. Clifford was one of those people that could not abide disorder. He only allowed material that he was working on to occupy his territory. He manipulated the image on the screen in careful, calculated movements, looking up occasionally at the large multi-coloured map on the wall above the desk.

The map of Lac La Ronge showed Highway 2 from the town of La Ronge southward. Across the bottom of the map, a highway connected to Highway 2 ran eastward. It was in this corner formed by the highways that Clifford now carefully scanned for indications of infrared heat. He'd been distracted at first by moose and deer and wolves but had learned to disregard their images. Smaller animals were easily distinguished. Rabbits and squirrels appeared as bright dots. Moose and deer were also easy to distinguish. Wolves however, caused him more frustration. Their infrared image required more scrutiny, to distinguish them from a human when they were lying down. When they ran single file in pursuit of a deer or moose, the wolves showed clearly on the screen. Clifford's main frustration was the forest canopy. Infrared images faded in and out as they moved through the forest, hidden under the canopy, then briefly emerging into clearings, only to disappear again.

He manipulated the image on the screen to focus on an area where a glimpse of an image disappeared. Spruce over a hundred feet tall filled the Bow River valley and formed an impenetrable barrier to the satellite scan. Something that generated heat disappeared under those trees before Clifford could identify it. He manipulated the focus, zoomed in and out, but the image was gone. He gave up and moved on, wondering if it might have been a human.

He often wished that he could observe for himself the territory that he scanned. The windowless trailer filled with equipment felt far too distant and out of place. If he could see the territory, observe the canopy and the terrain for himself, maybe he could make this work.

The presence of Inspector Spross caused Clifford to sit straight in his chair and keep his eyes on the screen while his supervisor paced behind him. Slowly, the tension built. Spross had not said a word of criticism. He had not said a word. Clifford's concentration collapsed. He got up with the pretence that he was getting a coffee that he did not want.

"Find anything?" Inspector Spross finally spoke as much a greeting as a question.

"Glimpses of nothing. At least the weather is holding."

"Its colder than a witch's heart out there. His heat signature should show up today. It's minus thirty-six."

"If he didn't have clothes on, maybe. The cold weather helps to see his heat, but you can bet that he is adding clothing that will hide him at the same time. Most heat is generated by the human head — about forty percent of the total. But if he's wearing a hat, it's covered." Clifford rattled on out of nervousness and a need to hear a voice, even if it was his own.

Charles threw the basketball up against the backboard and watched it glance off the rim and fall to the floor of the Friendship Centre gymnasium. Five consecutive missed shots. Except for Charles, the gym was empty. The youth evening program was not attracting people and Charles often spent much of each evening alone. As he walked to the corner to retrieve the ball, the door opened.

"*Tansi, Nosisim.*"

"I'm doing good, Uncle. What brings you here?" Charles rolled the ball in his hands as he stood in front of his great uncle.

"Come to talk to you about Jimmy." The straightforward reply caused Charles to unconsciously take a half step backwards.

Charles was saved further discomfort when the Director of the Friendship Centre called him to a private meeting. Ten minutes later he again faced Uncle Zach in the empty gymnasium.

"I think I just got fired." Charles told him. "The kids I'm supposed to supervise are afraid to come here. It's those *Wetiko* stories that're going around, I guess."

"Well, now, there's nothing in your way to keep you from looking after your brother."

"What do you mean, look after my brother? There's nothing I can do about Jimmy. That's up to the police."

"He's your brother, your family. Nobody else should take care of him. You came to me and asked about our traditional ways. Remember." Zach patted Charles shoulder. "You asked how we do things. Well, if your family member does something to someone else's family, it's up to you to put those things right again. If you refuse to do anything, you are as much to blame as your brother. Maybe that's why those kids won't come here. They know you're responsible. Kids understand these things better than adults sometimes."

"What'm I supposed to do?"

"Find him."

"Then what?"

"You'll know." Uncle Zach began to walk away. "Jimmy will probably tell you what has to be done," he offered as he left the gymnasium.

Joe McQuay looked out of his favourite window at the trailer that blocked his view of the lake. He wondered if they would take their equipment back South now that it was clear that Jimmy Tinker had outsmarted their technology. Joe looked back at his desk and his copy of the interview transcript.

Jacob Ross sat up on the hospital bed and repositioned his bandaged feet on a pillow. "I was lucky, I only lost one toe. They saved the rest."

"Tell me about the guy who took your boots."

"It was Jimmy Tinker."

"Are you sure?"

"I've known Jimmy and his family all my life. It was Jimmy. Surprised the shit out of me when he jumped out of the snow. I saw that shiny blanket and went to see what it was. Looked like it was just laying in the snow between the holes for my net. When I got close he jumped up wrapped in that silver blanket and started dancing around like he was crazy. He was kind of bouncing. He had one hand behind his back, one hand on the snow, and it was like he was bouncing on three legs." Jacob repositioned himself careful not to move his feet. "He would come close then quickly bounce away. I just stood there at first, too surprised to do anything. He was kind of circling me, bouncing up and down. His head kind of rolled around like his neck was made of rubber. That's what got my attention. His head. When he came close I took a kick at that stupid looking head. He was down low, too low to punch, that's why I kicked. He grabbed my foot and flipped me on my back. Well really, he flipped me all the way over so that my face was in the snow and he was on my back. Then, he took off my boots and ran away still wrapped in that silver blanket."

"It's a survival blanket," Joe explained. "We assume he got it from Rodney Thorson's survival pack."

"How can a blanket that thin keep you warm?"

"It doesn't have to be thick. It reflects body heat back to the person. Do you remember anything else?" Joe purposely changed the subject to avoid telling Jacob about the satellite that could not see Jimmy because of the survival blanket. Even though the satellite was useless, it was still classified.

"Not much." Jacob lay back. "The more I think about it, though, the more I'm sure that all that dancing and bouncing and rolling his head around was to suck me in to kicking at him. All he wanted was my boots. I really understand cold now. I walked four miles across the lake in my socks."

Joe looked away from the transcript and out the window. "Where was that mad trapper?" He had to reconsider his view of Jimmy Tinker. Until now Joe was of the opinion that, given time, Jimmy would turn himself in; that his inherent sense of honour and balance would force him to do the right thing. It was an opinion developed over decades in northern communities where the majority of crime was solved by the confession of a sober, sorry culprit. But Jimmy Tinker was something new. In the Southern cities someone might steal a person's boots if they were an expensive brand name. But in the North, that sort of crime would never be heard of.

No, Jimmy Tinker was not the ordinary case. What tugged at Joe's mind the most was that Jimmy was a trapper. A trapper would never steal someone's boots and leave them to walk in February weather. Maybe there was something to those *Windigo* stories. He would never admit to anyone on the force that he even considered the thought. He would be laughed all the way to an early retirement. But the other explanation that Jimmy might have rabies was wearing away. Even with treatment, rabies victims usually were dead in a week after the onset of symptoms. Rabies might be a horrible way to die. Victims usually experienced pain and terror, but it was a relatively quick death.

Joe looked away from his window, but the thought of Jimmy Tinker stayed in his mind. A rabies victim was usually disoriented, terrified, salivating and paranoid. Jimmy was smarter, stronger and not showing any loss of mental ability. Joe knew who to ask about *Windigo* stories. There was one person who would not laugh at him.

It would be good to visit with Dan Settee, listen to his stories and drink good coffee. For a moment Joe wished that he were part of the manhunt, out with Dan looking for a trail and away from the new formality of La Ronge, roadblocks and patrols. The military presence in the town did not have a great physical impact. There were only twenty-eight soldiers, a few trucks and jeeps. The occasional roadblocks on the highways were manned by pleasant, polite, and not visibly armed men and women in winter uniforms. The impact was psychological. La Ronge residents were not accustomed to the stress. Life here was far different from that experienced by Southerners. There is something about living in the trees that causes people to be laid back. The calm essence of the forest affects people over time. Even the most hyper new residents soon found themselves slowing down. Joe was one of those people. The excitement of the manhunt repelled him more than it attracted him.

Ground Search

Henry bit his tongue for the pain. Distraction from his rising need to thrust deep and reach down inside for release. Lois drew her lover deeper into herself. Opened her body to him, opened her heart and showed her soul to him. She felt Henry slow his pace and ease his thrust. It felt like he was rejecting her, like he was repulsed by her soul. Lois wrapped her legs around Henry's back and drew him back close, pulled him deeper into herself.

The blood taste in Henry's mouth made him ease the pressure of the bite. The need to breathe forced him to open his mouth and gasp for air. Too late to stop, he felt the first rush of release, the second and third pulsations that relieved the ache in sudden spasms of tension going to relaxation, to tension, to release, to tension, to pulsation.

Lois felt Henry's release within her and tried to pull all of him into her, into that place that was special to her. She wanted him to fill every part of her, to be where she was, to share the special place with her. She forced her tongue into his mouth. She was met with the salt of blood, with the assault of blood that rushed into her mind. Now it was Lois that pulled back and away from the violence of her lover's mouth.

Henry walked down the original street to the old fish plant by the lake. With the achievement of reserve status, Denare Beach had expanded and now consisted of two parallel streets that joined in a half loop at the bottom of the hill. He felt the wind in his face. A lonely wind that blew across the frozen lake.

Henry remembered an old woman who told him when the Cree language was no longer spoken, the wind would stop blowing.

Lois spoke perfect Cree. It was her primary credential as a Native Courtworker. Lois was behaving strangely after they made love this morning. Henry worried about his performance. Had he come too soon? No, it was more than that. Something more fundamental than unsatisfactory sex was bothering her, and Henry had no idea what it might be. He couldn't let it hang between them like this. He decided to return to the warmth of her cabin nestled in the pines beyond the Department of Natural Resources office.

"It's Jimmy," Lois told him. "I'm sorry Henry, but I can't seem to get it out of my mind."

"Get what out of your mind?"

"*Wetiko*. Cannibals."

Henry exhaled. He did not want to have the conversation that was coming. He did not want to speak about the horror of his brother with his newfound lover. Did not want to open himself to the pain of an honest discussion. But that was what Lois was insisting upon.

"What would it be like to eat human flesh?" She spoke the words that were the first steps down a trail that Henry did not want to tread.

Dan answered the knock on the motel room door reluctantly. He wanted to be alone when he phoned Mary. He was enjoying the company of Inspector McQuay, an old friend. But Mary would be going to bed soon and now someone else was at the door. Mary would understand a late phone call but she was getting older and deserved undisturbed sleep. Charles introduced himself to Dan. He knew Inspector McQuay from his many nights in the drunk tank and nodded hello.

"How did you know where to find me?" Dan asked.

"Your wife's cousin, Jean, told me."

Dan did not need to hear more. Like most connections in the North, this one was explained by family. He need not phone Mary. If she was talking to Jean she likely knew more than Dan. "I don't know how much help you can be in trying to find your brother. We had fresh tracks earlier today but we lost them."

"Whatever I can do," Charles stated as honestly as he could. "I don't have much, no ski-doo or snowshoes or really much outside gear at all. But I do know my brother and I would like to be there when you find him. I don't know . . . I guess I just want to talk to him."

"Don't worry about the equipment." Dan had been feeling guilty about his exorbitant salary. "I'll outfit you and pay you a decent wage to boot." He turned to Joe. "I'm not going to get any static from your department about hiring my own assistant, am I?"

Joe shook his head.

"Now here is what we are up against." Dan turned his attention back to Charles. "Help yourself to coffee in that thermos. Your brother is one tricky son-of-a-bitch. Like I said, we had fresh tracks this morning but by noon we lost him. He led me through some of the thickest bush out there and for no other reason than to give me a hard time. He wanted to show me what I was in for. He would go into those damn little Spruce going West and come out going East. He wasn't trying to lose me in there, cause he didn't hide his trail. How the hell he got through some of those places with those big snow shoes of his is just beyond me."

"Fifty-four inch Alaskans." Charles interrupted "He was pretty proud of himself when he got those."

"Alaskans are good snowshoes, good design for long distance. But fifty-four inch. How big is your brother?"

"'Bout the same as me. Five-eight, hundred and sixty pounds."

"He must have incredible legs. I would have guessed he was taller from the length of his stride, way taller." Dan paused in thought for a moment. "Holy shit! He has to be airborne to run like that. I found places today on the lake where his snowshoe prints were at least six feet apart. I thought I was tracking a giant." He rubbed his chin as he was in the habit of doing when in thought. "Like I said, we tracked him from where he took Jacob's boots, through that thick bush around Turtle Creek, and the Bow River. Then he went straight East across the lake to Fox Point. That's about twenty miles. He had to have been running, no, flying to leave tracks that far apart."

Dan was thinking as he spoke, his finger stroking his chin more rapidly now. "Those snowshoe tracks weren't very deep. You could hardly see them. Partly because the snow is hard pack on the lake and partly because he uses extra big snowshoes, spreads his weight over a bigger area, but even so, those tracks were light. If there had been any wind at all today they would have been covered up. Well, he didn't lose me on the lake. His tracks disappeared when he got onto a logging road down by Wapaweka. So tomorrow, Charles, you and I are going to walk that road, one on either side, until we find where he turned off. We'll have to check every Moose track or Wolf track to make sure he's not walking in their footprints. But if he can fly, we can't track him through the air."

Jesse's return home from jail did not turn out to be the wonderful thing he had imagined during the total six months of his incarceration. Home had been okay. His sister Gladys had done her best to welcome him back. But her anguish showed through her forced smiles. *Nokom* Jean seemed older than old. Quieter and sterner. Home had changed but it was still home.

School was a different story. Jesse faced the loud mouth grade eleven student, who was showing off in front of his friends, taunting the jailbird. Jesse simply responded, "It's not worth breaching probation to kick your ass." And walked away. But was it? What the hell was school, anyway? Even if he attended everyday in conformity with the probation order, that bitch counsellor had made it clear that it was unlikely he would pass grade nine. He had already missed too much school. How the hell was he supposed be in school and jail at the same time?

Henry skidded the truck to avoid the jaywalker. Rolled down his window to yell when he recognized the kid.

"Hey Jesse, where you going?"

"Nowhere."

"Jump in then and we'll go there together."

After Jesse climbed in, pulled off his toque and gloves in response to the truck's robust heater, Henry asked, "So, how was it?"

"Jail or school?"

"Well jail I guess, but school too if you want."

"I lived through jail, that's all I have to say about that. I guess I'll live through school too."

"I'm sorry."

"No need to be sorry." Jesse looked away. "You didn't send me there."

"I don't know what happened to Friesen that morning — six months incarceration and a year probation is tough for a first offence. I sure didn't expect that when I advised you to plead guilty."

"I guess you take what you get. I made it through jail. It was tough but it wasn't that tough." Jesse looked back at Henry. He appeared older, sterner than Henry remembered. "Tell you what though. Next time I steal a ski-doo I'm not going to try taking it back when I'm done. I'm going to strip that son-of-a-bitch down and sell the parts, make it worth six months . . . Just kidding, man. Shit, I'm clean, squeaky, know what I mean?" Jesse smiled and the young face that Henry remembered returned. "Tell me, what happened to Jimmy? He used to be good to me. Treated me like a real person, you know."

"What have you heard?"

"Same shit."

"Well he sure has a lot of people looking for him."

"Yeah, I heard that. Even Charlie, eh? Surprised the shit out of me. First, that good-time Charlie sobered up. But that he's working for the tracker, really fucked me up."

The sound of the fan blowing air through the truck's heater filled the silence for a long moment. Then Henry asked, "How's your sister?"

"Gladys, she's okay, I guess. She's at work. I was going to ask her for a ride home instead of taking the bus."

"I'll drive you there. I should go back to the office anyway. She still works at welfare?"

"Yeah, right next to where you work."

"I'd like to talk to her some time."

"What about?"

"Something Jimmy said."

"What he say?"

"He said he got her message."

Edward forced his body out of bed. A contest of will over fatigue, and will won. Every bone in his body ached; his nose was plugged completely, which forced him to breathe with his mouth open. The parts inside his mouth that were not dry were coated with a thick slime. His chest felt as though it, too, were filled with slime. Even his hair hurt.

"How you doing this morning?" the breakfast cook asked.

"Fuckin' rough."

"You look it. Lots of the guys have colds this week. Looks like a bad one is going around."

"Naw, it's just what happens when a cold comes underground. It's always cooler and damp down there. Just makes it hard to get rid of."

"Lots of vitamins man, lots of vitamins."

Edward didn't want to chat things up with the cook. He wanted a hot breakfast, orange juice, lots of orange juice, a coffee and a couple of cigarettes. Then he would go back into the damp dark of the mine. His cold would have to look after itself. Edward needed to work, needed to exert. But maybe he would stop by the nurse's station first.

"Go back to your room and lay down. You are not going to work today."

"It's only a cold." Edward argued with nurse Hazel. Hazel the witch. She was less than plain with round protruding cheekbones and a pointed chin. It was as though her face and body should have been much larger but someone had scrunched it all up into one small rumpled package. Hazel had no reason to pretend to be pretty or dainty and didn't.

"Bullshit. I have five guys with pneumonia going out on the plane already. Whatever is going around, I don't want everyone in the mine down with it. You are not going to work today. Give me a hard time and I'll phone the Mine Captain."

Edward complied, dutifully took the prescribed medication, and went back to bed. He did not have the strength to resist.

He woke two hours later, drenched in sweat, tangled and strangled by the covers. He clawed frantically to free the sheet from around his throat, threw it back and away. He was free from the sheet but he still could not breathe. He lay on his back and gasped for air. He battled the pillows into place under his shoulders to allow himself to sit up. The effort triggered a coughing spasm that produced a mouthful of phlegm and left Edward weak and faint.

Like anyone who works nightshifts, Edward had a heavy grey institutional blanket hung over the window to keep out daylight. He lay in the dark heat of his room. His sickness stunk. It coated his body, filled his nose and mouth and lungs. The sickness wrapped itself around Edward and drained his strength.

Northwind found Edward's window and tried to peer in. It wanted to know if he was ready to go, ready to let life go, ready to go dance with his ancestors. Edward was unaware of Northwind outside the triple panes of glass and the heavy blanket. Fear suddenly and unexpectedly rose up in him. Fear ignited a spark under his life drum. His heart's dull thud,thud increased tempo. This rapid drumbeat of life turned Northwind away.

The fear gradually left Edward's heart, slowly abated. The drumbeat slowed, found a steady pace, a rhythm of continuity. But the spark of fear that was drowned by his heart found fuel in Edward's mind. He sat on the edge of his bed, no longer able to lie down, afraid to assume the position of a corpse.

Edward was completely aware that he was going to die, perhaps not today, but someday. Then what? Would he be conscious, forever immobile, or would he pass away, fade to nothingness? What about the moments before death? Edward's mind raced, reversed, found a new path and raced again. What about the moment of death itself? Crushed by a slab of rock, blown to pieces by dynamite, drowned in a flooded shaft, smashed in a plane crash on the way home, never to see home again. Edward's mind put him in each situation of death and forced him to experience the moment of horror, forced him to look at his pathetic self.

Death danced through the neurons of his brain, pried loose imbedded convictions and left Edward adrift. Rationalization became impossible as each thought failed to find a base to build upon and had to be abandoned, left to swirl with other thoughts now categorized as nonsense. Finance, fortune, fame, reputation, strength, conviction, loyalty, worker's code, politics, champion, left right, surface underground, home and away, became meaningless or at least petty. Northwind had not touched Edward. Its mere nearness toppled the pillars of his belief.

Edward would have run to God or Jesus or whoever, but sister Evilyn stood in his way with a bath towel. Sister Evilyn, who forced him into a bathtub and scrubbed him with a brush, then fondled his testicles, forced her tongue into his mouth and then beat him for her transgressions. He sat on the edge of a single bed in a stark blackened bunkhouse room alone, without any comforts.

He forced himself to calm, got up and tore the blanket from the window for the light. He stood there for a moment blinded at the brilliance of sunlight on snow. Daylight for underground miners can often appear overly bright. Edward squinted as he looked out. Slowly his eyes adjusted and he watched the wind swirl snow through the thin pines behind the camp. He hadn't always been a miner — he remembered another bright sunny day.

Edward was one of the workers that left for Alberta in quest of a wage, a good wage. In the early days, hard physical work for Edward was more than income and livelihood; it was also art, self-expression and therapy. His first job in Edmonton was at a cement distributor. Edward's job was to load semi trailers with eighty-pound bags of cement. The first day he worked alone, with no one to tell him when or if he could take a break. By late morning, Edward's arms felt weak. He wondered whether he could finish the day. By noon, thirst dried his throat and caused each breath to burn. Edward kept working, one heavy bag at a time from the untiring conveyor belt to the stack at the front of the trailer.

The only person who spoke to Edward that entire day was the yard supervisor who explained how to stack cement bags, varying long with across to create a stable load. Edward was then left to carry bags from the conveyor end. The supervisor did not want an Indian on the crew and gave minimal direction. He watched from a distance to ensure that Edward kept working. The equipment operators took breaks, joked or argued, as was their mood. Today they laughed at the dumb Indian who did not know enough to stop for coffee or lunch.

By late afternoon, Edward found a place in his head where he could hide from the pain in his arms and shoulders. There was a spot behind his forehead. Edward stayed in that spot and ignored his pain, thirst and hunger. He no longer thought about the end of the day and rest. Edward thought about the moment and finishing the moment. Pick up the bag. Walk to the stack. Place the bag. Walk back to the conveyor. Pick up the bag. He felt the cement dust on his skin; felt the burn of lye where it reacted to sweat. He felt the burn of the sun on his arms and face and head. His sweat soaked his T-shirt and held the cement dust that burned into his skin. Edward's hair filled with dust and sweat and drained his mind. The heat made him dizzy and drew upon his strength. The sun tried to find its way into the spot behind Edward's forehead where he hid. Edward's body picked up a bag, tossed it to his shoulder, and walked steadily to the stack. Edward stayed in the spot behind his forehead and rested.

The sun slowly crossed the sky, increased in intensity at its height and eased gradually as it settled in the West. As the day progressed the yard supervisor and the crew gradually came to respect the Indian that worked all day in the sun without stopping for rest, or food or even a drink. After ten hours their respect turned to shame. Shame for not offering a drink of water, shame for taking turns eating their own lunch to keep the Indian working, shame for being out-worked by a lazy Indian. After twelve hours the yard supervisor shut off the conveyor belt and mumbled, "See you tomorrow morning" to Edward and went home along with a very quiet crew.

Edward came out of the space in his head, climbed down from the trailer and walked over to a bottle of Ginger Ale left by the forklift operator. The last of the day coloured the Western horizon as Edward rinsed the slime and scum from his mouth. The warm Ginger Ale soothed his swollen tongue and opened his tightened throat. Edward felt the evening light on his face, turned to the West and was filled with the beauty of the sunset. An intense feeling of greatness washed over him. His vision was perfectly clear. His mind was a crystal; his body was filled with the strength and agility of a Wolf. Edward's spirit sang. Never in his seventeen years had Edward felt greatness, perfect intensity or the power of manhood. He would never again experience such a moment of perfect triumph, though he sought it constantly. No drug experience would ever give this clarity of vision. Alcohol could never give this much happiness. Edward would never work hard enough to duplicate this moment, though he spent the rest of his life trying.

Reply

"What message?"

Jesse shrugged. His face told Gladys that he did not know any more than he had stated. She changed the subject. "How was school?"

"I survived."

"A little rough?"

"Nothing I can't handle."

The memory of her after-church soul shout into the wind erupted fully formed in Gladys' mind. She rewound the scene and let it play again, then again, before she went to her room to be alone, away from the connection to her little brother and her Grandmother who sat on the couch in front of a too loud television and stitched beads to leather.

"Jimmy heard me crying in the wind," she whispered into the silence of her privacy.

Memories of the connection Gladys thought had been severed rushed back to her, all those times she sensed his Spirit close to her. She remembered feeling expectant and aware before Jimmy's arrival. How minutes before his knock on the door she knew he was coming. How she knew over the course of months that he was all right, that the trapline would release him back into her arms. Gladys had not felt the connection in months. She could not remember the last time she felt it, or when for sure it went away. It seemed to have faded away without marking a precise moment of departure.

She felt for Jimmy's essence again, searched within herself for the place where he touched her, found nothing and reached out with her mind. Gladys concentrated upon Jimmy's image drawn from her memory, an image of the fine handsome man who laughed with her. The image formed readily enough without effort. But when Gladys tried to communicate with the image it smiled and faded. It was after all not Jimmy but only a conjured image. It had no power to respond. Gladys tried again, reconjured an image, and was dismayed when it again failed to respond.

Gladys sat beside her Grandmother. At first she pretended to watch the television tuned to APTN. But the images of Inuit games soon became uninspired background. She shifted her attention to Jean's beadwork, each glass bead held in its precise position on the leather moccasin tongue by a loop of linen thread drawn tight and invisible in the floral pattern.

"*Nokom*, remember you said that old people could talk to each other from far away."

"Uh huh."

"How did they do that?"

Jean put down her beadwork and took a slow drink of cold tea from the cup she had forgotten. Gladys's question had taken her by surprise. Jean was visiting long dead relatives and friends as she stitched bead to leather. She needed a moment to return, to place herself in the now. If Jean had heard the conversation earlier between Gladys and Jesse, she might have been more cautious in answering the question. But, she had not heard. She had allowed herself to drift away, to find comfort in the past. Jean's answer was, in part, an apology for that inattention.

"It was the way they lived, my girl. Those old people were connected to everything around them. They knew how to listen. They not only talked to each other, they talked to the wind and the plants and the animals. It was the same as knowing what the weather was going to be tomorrow. If a storm was coming. They just knew because they learned to listen."

"Listened to what? The sound of the wind or what?"

"Not like that, my girl. They didn't listen only with their ears. They knew how to listen with their hearts and with their spirits."

"How do you do that?"

"You have to give up your logic and believe what you feel. Those old people didn't have logic in their way. They didn't have to practice listening. It's the way they lived everyday, in tune with everything. It's also a very hard way to live; you have to be honest with yourself before you can look inside yourself. If you are not honest you can hurt someone, probably yourself."

"But I still don't understand how."

Jean took another sip of cold tea. She was back in the present completely and alert. "Why do you want to know these things?"

"Oh, I'm just curious."

"You have to be completely honest with yourself and walk in this world in a good way. Then you might learn how to listen with more than your ears." Jean was finished speaking.

The burning sensation in his inner thighs made Charles long for comfort while the ache in his Achilles tendons prevented him from stretching out his legs to relax. He sat in the middle of the couch with his feet on the coffee table and his head tilted all the way back because the couch was not high enough to support it. Exhausted, Charles wanted a cup of tea but did not have the energy to get up and make it. He wanted a pillow for his head but it was over there beyond his reach.

"How the hell did that old man walk so far, so fast?" he muttered into the silence of his living room.

"See you tomorrow." Dan's words of departure.

"If I'm alive." Charles' reply.

Charles had pulled off his boots and parka. They were still in a pile by the door. He looked away. If he did not see them he would not have to get up and put them away.

It was hunger that finally caused Charles to roll to one side for the leverage to force himself to his feet. It was hunger that held him up as he wobbled around the kitchen. He fried eggs, found a can of beans, a loaf of bread and a pound of butter with the foil peeled back to expose enough yellow for a knife. Dishes tomorrow. This first day would be the hardest. It was burned into Charles' memory. Decades from now he would recall it with perfect clarity.

Daniel could not help not smirking. He'd out walked a man half his age. He grinned as he remembered how Charles' pace slowed near the end of the day, how Charles slowly lowered his head and plodded. It was obvious that he forced himself one step at a time. It was not that Daniel felt any glee in Charles' suffering, not in the least. It was pity that called an end to the day while the sun was still well above the horizon. Daniel smiled to himself out of pride, pride in his ability and his age. But it nagged at Daniel as he settled himself comfortably in his motel room that they had walked better than twenty miles without finding any sign of the *Wetiko*.

That thought triggered another thought and a realization: Daniel was not tracking a human. He *was* trying to find a *Wetiko*. He shrugged. It would be the police officers who spent today in their suburban trucks who would have to put the handcuffs on whatever was at the end of the trail. The thought that was triggered was that he did not know what a *Wetiko* track looked like. None of the stories Daniel ever heard mentioned what a *Wetiko* track looked like. Wolverine, two by two like a big Mink. Wolves stepping in each other's footprints, even Big Foot with tracks like a human, but *Wetiko*? *Wetiko* could fly, couldn't he?

The thought drew on a memory, a story Daniel's Grandfather told only once.

"All I know is what I was told and what I heard for myself. My mom and dad left me alone while they went together to check the traps. All of a sudden my dad comes running home and a little while later my mom comes in. She told me that night that they were just walking together and a funny wind went past them. She said my dad told her to hurry home, that a *Wetiko* was after their son, and ran ahead. My dad never said anything to me. He just nailed up all the windows and got himself ready. When it was dark, my dad told me and my mom to stay in the cabin no matter what happened, and he went out. All night we heard them fighting. It sounded like a thousand birds all flapping their wings at the same time. The next day we moved away from there and never went back."

Daniel regretted that he never asked how his Grandfather's dad had prepared himself. It would be a good thing to know.

"*Petakwe.*" Charles shouted in reply to the knock on his door and was surprised when Henry entered. He had half-expected a neighbour or a neighbour's kid on an errand to borrow something. "The tea is still hot. Help yourself. What brings you this way?" Charles maintained his position on the couch with his feet on the coffee table. "Sugar? If there's none in the bowl then I'm out. You'll have to drink it like the old people, with a little bit of snow. Just watch for the yellow stuff out there."

"No thanks, I'll take it the way it is."

"Come over here and sit down where I can see you. I'm not going to move my ass off this couch. Like I said, what brings you this way?"

"Just checking on some rumours."

"Tell me."

"Heard you hired on to track Jimmy."

"Good old La Ronge gossip, faster than priority post. I just started today. Got hired yesterday."

"So when did you develop a sense of justice?"

Charles sat up. "Got nothing to do with justice. Not white man justice, anyway. I just want to be first to find Jimmy. I want to talk to him. What's wrong with that?"

"But you're helping the police and the army to find him."

"Somebody has to. He's pretty fucked up, don't you think? Anyway, the police probably *will* find him. Don't you think it might be a good thing if one of us were there when it happened?"

"What are you going to say to Jimmy when you do find him?"

"What the fuck is this? Cross-examination? I'll say 'hey bro, what can I do to help?"

"Easy Charles, I'm not here to run you over. I just want to know what's going on. That's all."

Charles eased back, relaxed again into the comfort of the couch. "What's going on is I'm trying to do the best I can with what little I got to help Jimmy and to live up to the responsibility of being a brother."

"Got ya."

"And I could use a little help. I need you and Edward in on this too."

"Whatever I can."

"Don't be so quick. We don't know where this is going. You make a big promise like that, you might have to keep it."

"I will. Lois and I have been talking a lot about my family and my responsibility. I'm beginning to realize some things and how important they are. I'm just not certain how to proceed."

"You know something? Whenever you don't know what you're doing, you start to sound like a lawyer. I don't know a hell of a lot either. But, I've been talking to Uncle Zach and he says we're responsible for Jimmy. In the old days we would have to make amends to the families of the people he killed to keep everything in balance. And I don't mean just balance between the families. We have to keep *everything* in balance."

"Everything?"

"I mean the sunrise and the sunset, winter, spring, summer and fall, the Earth, the Sky and every living thing in between. I mean every relationship we will ever have. I mean our children, our grandchildren, and so on for seven generations ahead and at the same time seven generations of ancestors behind us all depend upon our taking care of the responsibility that's been put on us."

"Big responsibility."

"Naw, all we got to do is our best."

"I don't get it. Why are *we* responsible?"

"'Cause he's our brother. We're the same flesh as him, the same blood. What happens to him happens to us. One of us gets out of balance, the rest of us have to put it right again."

Edward watched the wisps of cloud pass in front of a very bright full moon while he urinated in the snow behind Uncle Zach's cabin. The snow's reflection of the moonlight doubled the moon's intensity so that the night became almost as bright as day. But in the shadows of the thick Spruce forest beyond the cabin clearing where Edward now focused, night's darkness lay heavy between the black trees, ominous.

Edward felt his fear begin to rise. The darkness felt as though it were creeping toward him. He faced it. Looked into the shadows and rationalized his fear for what it was. Christian superstition. There was nothing evil in the night. Black is not bad; it is just black. Night is only the balance of day. He heard Zach in his mind. "To an Indian, everything comes from the Creator; Mother Earth and the Four Directions. Everything is good." Edward suddenly understood. Uncle Zach had not avoided Edward's questions about death as he told story after story, smiled, poured tea, laughed, told another story, patted Edward on the back and gently teased.

Cold seeped through Edward's clothes. The night air had freshness to it, cleanliness. Edward drew it deep into himself, exhaled, let a shiver shudder through him and returned to the warmth of the cabin. He wanted to tell Uncle Zach about his understanding but there was no need. Zach saw it in his eyes, in his face and in his walk. He walked in a good way. Edward did not have time to speak of his awakening because Uncle Zach began another story.

"I knew this man, used to live down the lake, other side of the big island. He went to the otherside. He was real sick one time and he drifted away. Said he had two helpers show him the way, one holding each shoulder. They were in outer space, way past the stars. They came to a wall of fire and the two helpers told him not to be afraid. He said they went through that fire and on the otherside was a beautiful place with lots of lakes and trees and everything was brand new over there. Then he kind of woke up in this world again and all his relatives were sitting around his bed. When he drifted off again, he tried to find his way back to that planet he had seen, but his relatives that died before came and stopped him. He said his Grandpa told him not to worry. That place would always be there for him but not yet. It was not the right time yet.

"That man died not long ago and at his funeral I was happy because he went to a good place. There's lots of stories like that. Me, I never seen the otherside. Don't want to, either, until it's my time. Heard lots of stories about the Northern lights. *Wawatew* we call them in Cree. Sometimes they'll come and get you. Stories like that. But I never once heard an Indian tell a scary story about the otherside. None of the old people, when I was young, were afraid of dying. They all seemed kind of happier as it got closer."

The next morning Edward awoke to the soft warm light of kerosene lamps and the delicate smell of frying bannock. "What's this anti-fur lobby they're talking about on the radio?" Uncle Zach wanted Edward's explanation of CBC's 6:00 AM news report about someone in Toronto arrested for spray painting a well known woman's fur coat.

"Some people think trapping is cruel. Animal rights and that stuff."

Zach thoughtfully turned the bannock in the bubbling lard. "What do they mean, cruel?"

"Well, leg-hold traps, I guess. Animals chewing their legs off to get out of traps, stuff like that."

Zach took a few more thoughtful moments, fished the bannock from the frying pan and set a plate on the table beside the lamp. "There's tea on the stove, *Nosisim*. Get this bannock while it's hot. You know I been thinking about this for a long time. Never told no one before. Didn't want to hurt anyone's feelings. But maybe we shouldn't sell them our fur anymore. Got nothing to do with this stupidity going on about cruelty. Only a real dumb trapper lets an animal chew its leg off. Most of the time I check my traps the animal is dead when I get there. I don't think he suffered too much when he died. Muskrats, Beaver, Otter usually drown when you catch them. First thing they do to get away is head for deep water. That's where they feel safe. A trapper knows this, sets his traps or snares so the animal drowns without a fight. Some animals don't fight the trap. You catch a Lynx and often he just sits and waits. Bear is the same way.

"Those people must think it is easy to trap animals. It's not. Nine times out of ten you don't catch anything. If the animal smells your trap he won't go in it; he'll steal your bait and laugh at you. When you catch something you got to skin it just so, and stretch it just so, and make sure you do a good job fleshing it without making a hole in the skin. I used to take pride in that stuff, when fur was worth a little bit. You could make a buck. Not anymore. But that's not why I think we should stop selling them our fur. It's about balance, *Nosisim.* The Indian's trouble started when we quit treating the animals like our brothers, when we forgot that the animals give themselves to us. We started to get into trouble when we sold our brothers for money and for whiskey. All of the hard time stories are after we sold our brothers. The stories from before that time tell about lots of animals, no hunger, no sickness.

"But you still trap, *Moshum.*"

"Little bit. Mostly out of habit, I guess. But I don't sell it like I used to. Nowadays I trap Muskrats and Beaver mostly for food. The pelts I like to give to the old ladies to make mitts and mukluks. You should see the nice Beaver jacket Jean made for me."

Escape

Northwind wove through the spaces between bare Poplar branches. It gently wrapped itself around Jimmy, eased under his survival blanket and tried to find its way into his parka, tried to find Jimmy's heart. Jimmy did not mind Northwind's intrusion. It was a gentle and kind seeking. The trail Jimmy followed was first walked by a Fisher who left his scent to be followed by Fox looking for Fisher's leftovers. Fisher followed the river, stayed in the tall trees of the deep Bow River valley, looking for Squirrels. Bear widened the trail, dug out stumps and ripped apart fallen logs in search of insects. Deer then chose the path and packed it with their hooves until it became a winding half hollow that other animals, and now Jimmy, would follow for as long as it headed in their chosen direction.

Out of habit, Jimmy paid attention to the tracks on the trail. He walked slowly, head down, not going anywhere other than South. The feeling that he was watched lessened in this direction. Jimmy's thoughts were as slow as his pace. Deliberately concentrated. He knew he was freezing to death. He no longer shivered. He felt warm and drowsy. Jimmy need only lie down and sleep and he would never awake again. But that was too easy. There remained within Jimmy a desire for life, a dim flicker that, despite its weakness, kept Jimmy on his feet and held his attention.

She waited beside the trail, the woman from the dreams. Jimmy stopped. She had changed now that she was in this world. The beauty was still there, or rather there were hints of it around her. The white dress was the same but now he could see the grease stains down the front. She was eating some unidentifiable leg of a medium-sized animal perhaps a Beaver. She held it out to Jimmy, an offer to share. He declined the offer with a weak single shake of his head.

She no longer held the power to attract Jimmy. He stood back. She had become larger, rounder. Her cheeks were fuller. Her eyes were sunk deeper. Her hair still shone, but now it was obviously oily. She continued to eat, nibbled on the bone, found a bit of gristle and crunched it. "You're almost there, Jimmy." She wiped the grease from her hand on her dress.

"Almost where?"

"To the land of plenty, my lover. To the land of plenty." She crunched down on the now naked bone, splintered it, delicately licked the marrow from its core, and then waved the remainder in emphasis. "My lover, you have only a few more steps and you can lay with me forever." She stepped onto the trail and began Southward. Jimmy followed. It was, after all, a continuation of his journey.

She finished the bone, picked splinters from her teeth with a fingernail, walked a few steps, snapped off a birch branch and nibbled on the buds, plucked each one off with her teeth until the branch was bare. Then she chewed off the bark, all the time walking gaily down the trail, swinging her arms, a bounce in her step.

She chewed the branch to nothing, snapped off another from a Willow as she passed and ate it too, as delicately and with as much pleasure as a Deer. She turned and smiled a long-toothed grin at Jimmy. She was much older than the woman in the dreams. Jimmy followed, one slow step at a time. He listened to his own breathing; experienced the slow rise and fall of his chest. This world in that moment felt small — only Jimmy, the woman and the trail. Even the tops of the trees overhead did not register in Jimmy's shrinking consciousness.

She finished the Willow and snatched a Squirrel. His chatter stopped mid squeak when her hand grabbed him off a low branch. A long thumbnail scraped the bush tail and exposed a bare sliver of flesh and cartilage. She peeled the pelt from the Squirrel in long strips like a banana. Squirrel stopped squirming before she licked the fatty juices from his warm carcass.

"JIMMY COME HOME." Gladys's heart and soul call hit Jimmy from behind and almost knocked him to the ground.

Inspector Rolf Spross enjoyed this part of his position. He began to prepare for the morning briefing shortly after 5:00 AM, the way an actor prepares for a performance or the way a lawyer talks to a mirror before he speaks his final arguments to a jury. Spross strode with what he hoped was apparent confidence in front of the gathered officers in the La Ronge detachment, occasionally he stopped and pointed at a large map. "We presently have the town completely contained. There is a military blockade on each of the highways. One here, north of the airport. One here, south of the sawmill, and one here, just south of what is called Far Reserve. That's the limit of the military's involvement. The remainder of the containment consists of snowmobile patrols on the trails and along the lake. We anticipate that he will return to town at some point. To our knowledge he has two brothers who live here, and a girlfriend. One of the brothers, Charles, is involved with the search and rescue experts that have been brought in to assist with tracking. He is *de facto* under surveillance. His other brother is a legal aid lawyer and for the most part is visible to officers. A third brother, Edward, shows up in town off and on, mostly off. When he is here he spends most of his time in local drinking establishments, and likewise, is easy to watch. The girlfriend,

Gladys Lonechild, lives on the reserve and has been very co-operative. We have every confidence that if Jimmy Tinker contacts her, she will contact the detachment. We have no one in town working under cover. There is no point.

"All indications to date are that Jimmy Tinker is hiding in the territory south of the lake and to the east. We have a continuous patrol of the roads and highways that mark the boundaries of the territory. Highway 2, here, marks the western boundary. Highway 165 marks the southern boundary and Highway 912, also known as the Wapaweka Road, runs north to what was a logging camp marks the eastern boundary.

"Now, gentlemen, I realize that the territory is massive, but it is almost impossible to subdivide. There is one road that runs up the middle. It's not much more than a trail. The snow has been bladed but patrols will still require four-wheel drive. We are going to concentrate on the eastern half. This is the area where he was last known to be.

"Now I will hand the remainder of this briefing over to Registered Nurse Rachel Quinn. We understand that James Tinker may have contracted rabies. For your safety, I have invited Ms. Quinn to explain from a medical perspective what it is that we are dealing with. Ms. Quinn."

Rachel nervously took the centre of the room. She was not an accomplished public speaker, and uniformed RCMP intimidated her. She planned to tell a joke in accordance with someone's, she could not remember whose, advice to loosen up the audience, but changed her mind and started speaking from the first page of her stack of material. "As anyone who has seen the movie *Old Yeller* knows — "

"Try *Cujo*," an officer interrupted. Rachel had never heard of Steven King's version of a rabid dog story. She looked around, puzzled, until her eyes met Inspector Spross who, with a gentle nod toward her material, encouraged her to continue. Rachel gave up on a conversational style and read directly from the page. "Rabies is a viral disease that can be transmitted from animals to humans. The disease is spread when the rabies virus enters the body through a bite, an abrasion, or the mucous membranes and attacks the central nervous system. Rabies in humans is rare. But once a person develops symptoms of the disease, death is inevitable. Antiviral therapy to treat rabies, once established infection occurs, is not available. Rabies prevention must remain the primary goal because the disease is always fatal once symptoms develop."

"So if he bites me, I'm dead." Corporal McKercher leaned forward. The hard plastic and aluminum chair scraped against the floor with a sound that set his teeth on edge.

"No." Rachel's bright green eyes looked up from her pages. "Symptoms do not develop immediately. The disease has an incubation period the length of which depends upon . . . " She looked down again, flipped pages, "the particular strain of the virus, the condition of the host, the amount of virus transmitted, size of the bite, and the distance from the site of entry to the brain. The incubation period can last from weeks to years but is usually one to three months. The victim does not experience signs or symptoms of the disease during the incubation period. The only successful treatment of rabies must occur immediately following exposure, long before the onset of symptoms."

"So what are the symptoms? What are we looking for here?" Inspector Spross prodded.

"Well." Rachel flipped pages, found a spot and marked it with a finger. "Early signs and symptoms include malaise, fatigue, dizziness, an inability to swallow, fever, sore throat, productive cough, shoulder arm and back pain, weakness, abdominal pain, vomiting, severe headache, severe anxiety, visual hallucinations, and slurred speech. Later, the victim will experience hyperactivity, disorientation, hallucinations, bizarre behaviour, fever, and headache. The patient may have periods of hyperactivity alternating with periods of calm when the patient is cooperative and lucid but anxious." Rachel knew her voice sounded remote as she read directly from the page. She just did not have the courage in that moment to look up. She was too aware of her own beauty, her long red hair that caped her shoulders, her slender build and the blouse that emphasised that build. Her attractiveness betrayed her. It did not give her the confidence she sought when she carefully applied her makeup that morning. It distracted her. "Hypertension, hyperthermia, and hypersalivation also occur during this period." She continued to read rapidly, head down. "Drinking causes spasms of the pharynx, larynx and diaphragm, which causes choking, gagging and the classical hydrophobia. Patients may also experience hyperesthesia and priapism.

"Explain." Inspector Spross did not intend his request to sound like a command, but it did.

"Well . . . " Rachel paused.

"Please explain hydrophobia, priapism and hyperes . . . "

"Hyperesthesia," Rachel continued, "is being abnormally sensitive to stimuli. Hydrophobia is the fear of water, and priapism . . . " she felt herself redden despite her conviction that she was, after all, a medical professional discussing medical terminology "is a persistent erection."

Joe McQuay felt Rachel's discomfort and moved the agenda forward. "So what should we do if we do come into contact with suspected rabies?"

Rachel smiled for the first time that morning. "Well." She flipped pages. "Wash the bite for ten minutes with soap and water. Immediately contact your health care provider or go to your hospital emergency department. The healthcare providers may decide to give you several shots to prevent rabies. The shots are not painful. You should see your healthcare provider as soon as possible, but you should report any bite or possible exposure even if it occurred some time ago because the shots will still be affective as long as they are given before you develop symptoms of the infection." Rachel looked up from the page, the last page; she was finished and had not fainted or embarrassed herself. She felt herself breathe again, maybe for the first time since she began. The air filled her, slowed her racing mind, and Rachel was able to walk confidently from the room knowing that appreciative eyes followed her.

Jimmy stopped, stood flat-footed and watched the woman walk down the trail. She finished Squirrel, crunched the last tiny bones, licked her fingers and began to look around for something else to eat — Spruce gum, Labrador Tea leaves, Old man's Beard moss. She knew all the foods. Jimmy could learn from her. But Jimmy already knew far more than any man alive today. He knew the trail that led to the otherside. He knew the taste of death. He knew the smell of blood, fresh before life faded and it grew stale and still. He knew the vibrance, the rush, the free flow of another's life flow into him. Knew the weakness of humanity and the strength of the taker.

Follow her down this path to personal power, or answer Gladys. But why? Gladys was soft and weak, one of the pitiful. She cried in her sorrow, felt the pain of loss, blubbered words of departure through tears and snot, wiped her eyes with her sleeve and tried to smile. Jimmy turned North to the only place he knew on Earth where there was kindness and pity for him.

Going home always seems faster and smoother than leaving. There is in going home a tug, a draw that pulled Jimmy, held him on his feet and fed him. Jimmy heard Charles laugh. Thought it must be his imagination and pushed forward. The deeper sound of Daniel's laughter snapped Jimmy still. He stood motionless on the trail, alert, ready. The Bow River lay to Jimmy's left, Westward. Ahead to the North the voices. To the East a very steep climb, then a Pine forest mixed with Spruce, logging roads and overgrown clear cuts. Behind Jimmy to the South she walked and ate.

Jimmy chose West, six steps to the river, one step on a fallen log and across. From upstream, Dan's attention was drawn by the motion and he glimpsed Jimmy enter the Willows on the opposite shore. He crossed on the same log moments later with two steps. Charles took four, as did the two officers behind him.

Jimmy's choice of West was based on memory. In 1979 Jimmy helped fight a huge forest fire that had started fourteen miles away and, with the assistance of Conservation Officers, managed to reach the river. Today Jimmy thanked the officers who had handed out boxes of matches to the firefighters with instructions to begin backfires. By noon of the first day the backfires were out of control. Jimmy and the other firefighters had constant work and income for the next two months before the fire finally burned itself out.

The burned forest lay in tumults of deadfall. Broken by wind they piled like a giant pick-up-sticks game, waist high. The Pine forest grew back thick. Each tree in competition to reach the sun. They filled the gaps between the fallen trees, thick as the fur of a giant beast.

Dan cursed under his now gasping breath as he fought his way through, climbed over fire-hardened logs with stiff unforgiving branches that gouged like wire barbs. The new growth was much more supple, even in winter, but its thickness impeded as branches grabbed and dragged against Dan. He momentarily lost sight of the tracks when a branch swept across his eyes. Officer McKercher pushed past Dan. This was his job, his duty. He did not need a tracker. The footprints ahead were clear in the snow. More importantly and more urgently he could hear the occasional *crack* of a branch as Jimmy fled. Like a novice hunter behind a wounded Deer, Leon McKercher smelled blood and rushed for the kill, high on adrenaline.

Officer Owen Bradley fell further and further behind as he tried to fight his way through the thick tangle of brush and deadfall. The radio he carried was not designed for the distance he wanted to transmit across. He stopped again and repeated through gasps the co-ordinates and direction of the chase, glad for global positioning systems; he would hate to have to use a map and compass in this terrain.

Charles followed the tracks of Jimmy, Daniel and Leon and simply stayed ahead of Officer Bradley. He was a mixture of emotions, wanting to see his brother and wanting him to run. He half wished Jimmy would lose them.

Daniel followed close behind Leon and wished Leon would not step on Jimmy's footprints. Even Wolves who run in each other's tracks know enough to run on each side of the prey's. Leon was messing up the tracks and Daniel was having trouble deciphering them.

Jimmy quit trying to think his way out and just ran, jumped over fallen trees, charged through the dense green. He fell, scrambled to his feet and lunged forward in a crouch. His head hit the log he was trying to pass under and he fell back. He sat for a full second flat assed in the snow, stood, shook himself off, threw off the silver blanket, walked five deliberate steps and began to run again. He stepped onto a log and gingerly ran its length, jumped off, found a log laying North and ran its length. "Like a Lynx," he thought and tried another log that ran West. Much easier than trying to climb over them.

Corporal Leon McKercher stopped. Unsure, he turned to Daniel. Daniel stepped aside to look for the trail ahead. Nothing. Shit! He had been following McKercher; now he would have to circle back to find where Jimmy turned off.

The cribbage board clattered to the floor. Its sound drowned out by the growing *thrump thrump* as the helicopters brought their engines up to speed. Three teams of standing-ready RCMP officers grabbed gear and evacuated the hanger where they had waited, played cards and practised techniques for weeks.

Jimmy continued to run, dodge and zigzag from one deadfall to the next. He intended to continue Westward, but found most of the dead trees that became his elevated trail lay North and South. A strong North wind that felled most of the burned trees twenty odd years ago turned Jimmy's path of escape. He ran mostly North.

The pilot of the lead helicopter set a course for the co-ordinates dictated to him by central command, made a very slight movement of the touchy control stick, levelled the helicopter off and headed for a position one kilometre west of the last known position of the fugitive.

A memory tugged at Charles. He stopped. Officer Bradley stepped past him. "I'm going to try to go around," Charles informed the back of the dark blue parka with the gold insignia, and returned down the track.

"Walk only in my footprints." Daniel's voice betrayed his annoyance. Corporal McKercher stood aside while Daniel searched the snow-covered ground. At first, Daniel missed where Jimmy ran down the log. Fifteen minutes later, after a couple of fruitless circles he, Leon McKercher and Owen Bradley were again on Jimmy's trail.

The three teams of standing-ready officers bound by the thin aluminum shells of vibrating helicopters found release as they rappelled down nylon lines into the forest. Sergeant Cliff Thompson took command of the eighteen officers assembled amid the deadfall and thick new growth. He was amazed that everyone was standing. No broken legs from hard landings, no one pierced by fire-hardened branches. "Everyone all right?"

he asked to no response. "Okay then, spread out. Form a line north and south. He should be here in a few minutes." Officers shouldered their weapons, adjusted straps, and began to work their way into the trees and brush.

Sergeant Thompson answered the urgent radio call. "This is air one. Go ahead tracker."

"The fugitive has turned north." The radio crackled back at him. "Repeat. The fugitive has turned north." Sergeant Thompson was not paying attention as Corporal Bradley gave new co-ordinates. He stared upwards at the hovering helicopters. Getting out was not difficult. They had simply obeyed the law of gravity. Getting back in would be a totally different proposition. He made a decision and acted upon it.

"Give me those co-ordinates again. Hey, Jim, get over here with that GPS. Boys we have some running to do."

Jimmy sensed the three teams of police officers as a presence somewhere slightly behind and to his left. The pressure of the sensation pushed him slightly to the right as it urged him forward. He skipped onto a fallen tree that pointed its blackened tip nearly Eastward, danced its length, hopped off, dodged through thick growth, found another pointed more Northerly and danced again.

It took a little time until Daniel fully understood Jimmy's method of travel. Tracks do not show up on deadfall. He put the puzzle together from the few tracks between the tangles. He could not track Jimmy at the same speed that Jimmy could travel. While Jimmy skipped and danced from one deadfall to the next, Daniel was forced to stop and look for tracks, occasionally following a deadfall in the wrong direction.

Jimmy's new heading toward the Northeast did not become obvious until Officer Bradley had checked and rechecked the GPS several times. Direction in thick forest without the assistance of Sun, Moon, Stars or technology is metaphysical, intuition. Daniel's deep Earth connection centred him on the Earth's surface. He remained always on the cross lines between four ancient Grandfathers. Even though Daniel might not know precisely where he was in any given minute, he knew where he was in relation to the four directions. It was simply that no one asked.

Charles retraced his way back to the river and up the ancient path along its edge. Sometimes running, sometimes walking quickly, he had time to question his spontaneous decision to try to go around. Doubt overtook him. There was nothing to assure him that Jimmy would be where he anticipated. There was only a path, a forest, snow and a memory.

Inspector Spross took complete control of command. GPS co-ordination between the officers on the ground, the helicopters and command central, provided all of the information on which to make decisions. The fact that all of his mobile force was now on the ground and unable to re-access the helicopters was something that had to be dealt with. He had at his command other forces, though not as mobile. He contacted the officers in charge of the army unit to seal off the northern boundary, and ordered every available officer with a truck, car or snow machine to converge on the area.

The North has no streets to blockade, no grid to cordon. Abandoned roads are soon clogged with willow or barricaded by fallen trees. Game trails criss-cross and lead apparently nowhere. Off the roads and trails, travel choices are between difficult and more difficult. Willow and closely growing spruce can be impassable except for a rabbit or a moose mad with rut. Inspector Spross soon discovered that he would need thousands of men, all familiar with the territory, to surround Jimmy. The territory was too vast, contained too many possible routes of escape, and was too thick to penetrate. His air support was blinded by the forest canopy as each tree spread its arms in prayer to sun, wind and rain. The canopy in winter is doubly thick as trees hold tons of snow, balance large chunks on delicate branches, or layers on broad boughs.

Jimmy's Northeast travel brought him to a road overgrown with Willow. Only the lines of the road remained where the ground was still packed too hard to allow life. He turned East and ran, his mind empty, his emotions flat.

She found him again. The woman ran through the trees to Jimmy's right. Unimpeded by deadfall, snow or thick growth. She loped easily, gracefully. "Where are you going, my lover?"

"Home, I think."

"Your home is with me now. There is nothing left in town for you."

"Leave me alone. I just want to go home."

"I'm not stopping you. Go to the town. Feast there. Maybe I will come eat along with you. Children. Children are tasty. Yes, Jimmy, let's go to town together." She faced Jimmy, running backwards — or maybe she was just floating ahead of him. "I will take my other form. My flying form and chase the children and you can catch them." She wiped the spit from her chin with the back of her hand. "Soon, my lover, you will pass to your other form. Like a butterfly you will leave your ugly weakling body and rise and fly and feast. But be careful, my lover. You are still a weakling. They can kill you. Not that any of them know how anymore. They are weaker and dumber than ever."

She spread her dove white wings, inhaled deeply. The frosted air passed through her skeletal body and fluttered the shreds of ancient leather that was once a white dress. She called down to him. "We will feast on children tonight, my lover." She banked left, let the wind catch her wings, and soared North.

Jimmy slowed to a fast walk. The overgrown road crested a hill and began to descend steeply. The sensation of a presence behind him diminished as he re-entered the valley of the Bow River. The memory that pulled Jimmy cleared as he viewed the terrain. A sawmill, lumber piles, camp, summer work, Charles, Edward and even Henry for a short while, salvaging logs, large naked and blackened Spruce from the valley bottom. The work, the camp, and the reunion of brothers lasted until most of the big burned trees were cut. Then, after the easy wood was taken, the owners moved the sawmill, presumably to somewhere equally profitable.

"Hey Jim."

Jimmy snapped around, the rifle wheeled on its sling, the barrel levelled on Charles' chest. Charles stepped back, hands away from his sides. "Easy Jim, I just wanted to say hello."

Jimmy lowered the rifle. "Hello."

"So what were you doing, just standing there staring at the sawdust pile like no one was chasing you?" Charles lowered his arms and carefully stepped closer.

"Just remembering old times. That was a good summer."

"Not worried about the cops?"

"Not really. Are you?"

"Not me." Charles shook his head and his eyes lowered slightly with the shaking. "I'm sorry Jim. It was me that found your trail. I was helping to find you."

"No shame in that Charles."

"I needed to see you."

"So you see me." Jimmy lifted his arms and turned slowly around as if to exhibit his clothing, which consisted of a worn green parka, wool pants crusted with snow, a Muskrat hat and new boots. When he again faced Charles, Jimmy's face was transformed into a broad smile.

"It's all right, Charlie. Hey do you remember when we worked here? Edward was trying to outwork everyone in camp and Henry couldn't take two steps without tripping. Remember that? Henry did good, going to university. He sure as hell couldn't work in the bush. You know, I wish I had told him more that I was proud of him."

"Jim, the cops will be here soon." Charles spoke with urgency. Jimmy looked back the way he had come.

"Naw, not for a while. Hey, you remember Flora?"

"What's with you? Still trying to tease me about Flora after all these years. Shit Jim, you're in serious trouble. The cops are going to catch you."

"I don't think today. They're too fat and slow. But what about you Charlie? How you doin'?"

"Colder'n fuck is what I am. Thanks for asking, asshole." Charles smiled back at his brother and felt his tension ease. "You son-of-a-bitch. Every cop in Saskatchewan and half of Canada's Army are looking for you and you just stand there without a care in the world." Charles removed his gloves and blew on his fingertips.

Jimmy stepped toward his younger brother reaching forward. Charles watched the bare hands approach and stood stock-still. Jimmy messed Charles' hair with one hand and pulled up his parka hood with the other. "Keep your head warm and your hands and feet will be okay."

"Still the big brother, eh, Jim?"

"Always, Charlie, and don't forget it. I'm going to ask you for a big favour soon, a big favour. But I have to ask Henry and Edward at the same time."

"Anything, Jim."

"Don't be quick, you might regret it."

A moment of silence followed as each brother tried to look into the soul of the other. Jimmy re-slung the rifle, adjusted the straps of his pack with a shrug, stepped around Charles and trotted on down the road. He crossed the river where the bridge once spanned, and disappeared from Charles' view around a bend in the road.

Zach pulled down on the Otter pelt to tighten it against the fleshing pole. Short firm strokes with a sharpened bone peeled the tight layer of fat and flesh from the pelt and left the white hide clean and smooth with only a greasy sheen. "Bone is still the best, faster than even the best knife and you don't have to worry so much about putting a hole in the hide. See here, this white line around the belly, that's from the snare. I caught this guy in one of my Beaver sets. If I were after Otter I would have made the snare smaller to catch him around the neck. I don't mind to catch an Otter once in awhile, they eat the Beaver; well, they eat the baby Beaver. I don't think an Otter has much chance against a big Beaver. Ever come across a Beaver on land or on the ice?"

Henry shook his head.

"Well, you don't want to. They'll attack, and them big front teeth are as sharp as hunting knives. You'd think them fat buggers would be slow. But I tell you they can move and jump. Killed me one once with a stick when it attacked me. It was about this high in the air." Zach indicated with the fleshing bone, chest height. "If I hadn't clubbed him, he'd a had me. Here, pour an old man a cup of tea." Zach offered an empty cup to Henry then continued with his work on the Otter pelt. "This woman you're seeing, Lois. Do you know her family?"

"Not much." Henry admitted. "I know she was raised by her grandparents and spent most of her life on a trapline."

"Hmm. From everything you said she sounds like a good woman. Too bad you never got to see how a healthy family works. You wouldn't be here asking an old man about relationships with young women. I can tell you some things I know, but it's mostly up to you, the choices you make. Keeping a relationship is the hardest thing in the world. You have to work on it every minute. And like everything else in this world, a lifetime of work can be destroyed in two minutes. A simple rule you have to remember. A woman can leave you any time and there is absolutely nothing you can do about it. You see lots of times someone will try to keep their partner from leaving. That's when things usually get really bad. Sometimes someone dies from that. The old teaching for us men is that we are to treat women with kindness and pity. That's how we keep a woman. But, you never let your woman come between you and your brothers and you never say anything bad about her family. If she leaves you, she has to go back to her family. So be careful you don't put anything in the way of that."

Zach cleaned the fleshing bone on the piece of canvas covering his lap. "You know the story about not talking to your mother-in -law, and when she comes to visit you're supposed to leave the house. That's what that's about, not coming between a woman and her family. But at the same time be careful she doesn't come between you and yours. Your family is your blood. It's forever. You can't break that." Henry felt Zach's eyes pierce him. "With your partner its different. She can leave you. If you remember all the time that she can leave any time she wants and there's absolutely nothing you can do about it, you will probably stay together because you will always be working to keep her. Kindness and pity. Remember that."

Henry nodded. "And keep praying right?"

"No!" Zach looked over the fleshing pole directly at Henry. "Don't get that mixed up. You can pray for your partner, but never pray to keep her. The Creator has no business between a man and a woman. It's their choice. It has to be their choice for it to work. And when it works there is nothing like it in the world. When a man and a woman come together and walk together they can find their balance. When you have balance in your life everything comes easy. You're not fighting against nature then. The hard part about walking the Red path is keeping that balance once you find it. Not just balance between you and your partner. You have to keep balance between you and your family and your community. You never ask the Creator to come between you and your woman and you never put another person there, either. You see, lots of times when people are breaking up they pull all their friends and family into it. That should never happen. It's their choice to be together or not to be together. It's nobody else's business. Getting other people involved only spreads the imbalance and makes things hard for everyone. There . . . "

Zach made a final stroke with the bone and the last of the fat and flesh from the Otter pelt fell into his lap. He picked it up. "See this, render this fat down and you get a very fine oil. Good for your hair. Makes it shiny and thick. Best thing for split ends." Zach flipped his braids. "See, the tips don't look like beaten up paint brushes. It's strange you coming here. Edward was here the other day and Charles has been coming around all winter. I guess it's all part of everything coming back to me. I should have been around more when you guys were young. It all works itself out. I just can't help but feel Jimmy is going to walk down the path next." Zach stood and stretched. He shook the Otter pelt so the tail flipped a few inches from the floor. "Anyway, give me a ride to town. I think I'm going to break my rule and sell this Otter. There's a few things I need around here."

Mary stopped the knife mid-peel. Her Mother's voice was still clear in her head. "Don't be cutting all the potato away, just take the peel off." She looked around her kitchen: electric stove, electric fridge, cupboards with doors. It was far from the kitchen of her Mother: wood stove, wood box, a few nails to hang pots and pans and cups, a shelf for plates. Her Mother's fridge was a snowdrift. The crispness of her Mother's voice began to fade in Mary's head. She sought to keep it. Replayed it again, then again. With each replay it dimmed more and more until it became Mary's voice. She let it go and quickly finished peeling potatoes. Now the peel was much thinner. Just because she lived without want didn't mean she had the right to waste. As she continued her preparations, Mary returned to her childhood and the warmth and laughter of the little log house just off the portage.

It was a busy house: two parents, five children and almost daily visitors. Someone new to play with everyday. Constant news, like living at the centre of the universe. Mary saw thousands of canoes inverted upon shoulders carried across the portage. Over the course of years, Mary had also seen tens of thousands of dogs pulling sleds for trappers, traders and even mail carriers.

She looked quickly at the kitchen clock — only four-thirty. Daniel would not be in his motel room until after eight. She thought of calling his cell phone but could not think of a reason important enough to justify the expense.

Mary lied to Mark when he came in from running his Grandfather's dogs. "Supper is on the stove, help yourself, *Nosisim*. I've already eaten."

Mark served himself. There was a lot left. "Are you sure you've eaten, *Nokom*?"

"I already said I did. Who are you to question me?"

Mark ate a mouthful in silence with his head lowered. Then he sat up a little straighter, found some courage. "Sorry, *Nokom. Moshum* said I was to make sure you ate while he was gone."

Mary did not respond. She did not dare. In that moment she was being wrung, shaken and left to dry by her emotions. The boy had done nothing to deserve her wrath. She would keep her silence, swallow the surge of anger and remember to appreciate the exceptional boy, the gift to an old woman.

The Grump had found a spot for itself centre, behind her breast, between her lungs. It moaned softly and sought to make Mary cry. It pulled dread thoughts into her mind and she almost ran away with them. She fought back against the Grump, pushed it away. Mary fixed herself a small plate and joined her grandson at the table. She could not afford the luxury of a Grump. Being a Grump can result in a pleasurable diversion, as Mary knew well. She just did not enjoy the cleanup required when it ended. Why couldn't that old man be here at home where he belonged, to make sure she ate — and she could make sure that he ate.

Daniel suddenly wanted to be home with Mary. The need surprised him, that he could feel her call in the middle of a chase. Adrenaline usually silences — perhaps the rapid drumbeat drowns out anything beyond heart, lungs and legs. Daniel kept his mind on the tracks in the snow ahead of him. He put Mary aside with a promise to the wind that he would phone tonight.

Lois watched from the back of the courtroom as Judge Friesen listened to the Crown and Defence alternate. The exchanges were quick, efficient motions, adjournments, pleas, "Guilty, your honour." And "Beg your indulgence, your honour." And "If it please, your honour." Lois wished Henry were in court this morning. Not that court would be conducted any differently.

She just wished he were there. She missed the way his back filled the fabric of a suit.

It was strange that she should miss Henry when it was at her urging that he took time off work to speak to a man. Lois had patiently explained Cree concepts to him. He was an eager student, quick to grasp the simplicity that tied everything together. But some old teachings are for women from Mother to Daughter, or more usual and true for Lois, from Grandmother to Granddaughter. Lois urged Henry, with gentle suggestion, that he seek a Cree man with understanding — *nistotamowin* — self-understanding, to explain those concepts peculiar to men.

Lois resisted being Henry's teacher. If she and Henry were to be partners neither could be superior to the other. Neither could be teacher. As Henry explained Euro legal concepts, Lois explained Cree understanding. They found a balance point. A place where they were equal.

Gladys put herself into the work that was always available. Social Services had been busy, especially in the North. Governments of both stripes have demanded the department perform more on ever shrinking budgets. As a secretary, Gladys was at the bottom of the work pyramid. For every child abducted by child protection workers a mass of required documentation found its way to Gladys's desk. Applications for assistance and denials of assistance and prescribed regimens for parents seeking the company of their children and department responses to parents created a paper and digital world that Gladys was able to hide in. In this world, she did not hear Jimmy's whispers of love to the wind as he ran with lengthened stride, pushed his legs to cover ground.

Jimmy was coming home. He felt ecstatic. Everything was coming to an end. He could see the finish. The clouds were moving aside. The Sun would soon shine again. The despair of this morning vaporized. Today was after all a change of the Moon. The Moon when trees crack in the cold finished and the Moon when Eagles return began. Jimmy laughed suddenly, loudly; he pulled strength from the sound, then put his mind back to his stride.

Jean felt something coming. The feeling grew all afternoon, a nag at the back of her mind. She cleaned her house, made a large bannock, put on a pot of tea and waited.

Edward did not feel tired. The last nightshift of the week was finished and he sat in his bunkhouse room. Usually he tried to grab a few hours sleep before the plane left at noon. Was he flying *out* or *in*, he wondered? *Back*, he decided, *back* to the world. Today was home day, fly day, as some of the miners called it.

This morning was different. The whole week had been different. Everything had gone smoothly, easily. Even though Edward had not put a lot of effort into his work, at the end of the week he had an average amount of production. He would earn his normal bonus, and bonus did not matter so much anymore.

Something nagged at him. Words tumbled in his mind. Edward found pen and paper and let the words out.

Grandmother's bones
Stones water dirt
Bacteria roots life
Ancestor's atoms swim
Surface
Climb stalks
Speak again
And again
To the Sun.
I am them

Old Old Ones
In Berries,
In Nuts.
I am them
In Moose meat
In Fish
In Corn
In Beans
In Squash
I am them
Again
I am the Water
Grandmother's tears
I am the Flood
In me
In the Beginning
I am the Rain

I am Sunshine
Since let there be light
I am Life
I am Fire
I Love
With all that I am
With all that I have
This Body
This Earth
Since then
Now
Tomorrow
My Bones in Dirt
Feed Grandchildren
Future.

Edward felt release as he placed the period at the end of the poem. The words had come out. He went down to the cafeteria for a coffee. On the way back to his room he passed the camp office and without thinking stepped in and changed his flight destination from Prince Albert to La Ronge.

Back in his room, Edward reread his earlier poem. He did not rationalize his changed flight plans. Did not concern himself that his car was parked at the Prince Albert airport. He was content that the change felt right. More words were tumbling in his mind demanding that he finish, that he make balance. Edward complied. Slowly at first, with long thoughtful pauses, then the words flowed from the pen.

Take Me Back
Do not bother to Cremate me
Spread my ashes from an airplane
I have no desire to fly
Along time from now
When I die
I have no cryonic hope
Do not freeze and keep me
Do not launch me into outer space
I have relatives among the stars
But I have never met them
I fear I would be lonely in that deep deep dark
Do not bury me at sea
When I was there I prayed only for shore
Give me back to my Mother
I am from her
Ashes and Dust and Mud
Lay me upon her bosom
Let me meet Raven
When he comes for my eyes

Let my crawling relatives
Carry me back from where I came
Leave my skull to grin at the sky
Let the Earth absorb me
Take me back
I will rise again
In Grass and Trees and Green.

Edward stood, stared at the inked page and said aloud to the empty room. "Now where the hell did that come from?

A light snow began to fall as Henry and Uncle Zach approached La Ronge. It was too cold for a heavy storm. The day had only warmed to minus twenty-five. Zach was quiet and had been since they passed through the last army blockade at the junction of highways 165 and 2 North. Now he spoke: "I'll go to Jean's. Been a while since we had a good visit."

"You can stay at my place if you want," Henry offered.

"Naw, it's all right. I like it at Jean's. Did you know her and I've been friends since residential school?"

"What residential school?" Henry had never thought of Uncle Zach in school.

"It burned down about 1949 or so. Used to be up the hill from the beach. Wasn't much in La Ronge those days — the Anglican Church, the school, Hudson's Bay Post and some Indians. I met Jean there. We kept each other sane. Jean's a good woman." Zach seemed to have trouble pulling his thoughts together, or he was being cautious about how much he said. He caught Henry's quizzical look and answered with a little smile. "Jean is my spirit sister. Her and I balance each other."

The image of Lois opened with a smile in Henry's mind.

"When we were in that school, they tried to hammer Christ into us. Jean was one of the older girls and she looked after me,

160

sort of as much as she could I guess. Every time after church she took me aside and told me stories. Most of them I already knew. She just reminded me with those stories that I was an Indian. I did the same for her when she was having a hard time. Jean understands. She was born with a gift. I have a little bit of a gift, too. Over the years we found how to use our gifts together." Zach let his hand run over his green packsack. "That's all."

At 8:07 PM, the phone in Daniel's room rang. He was expecting Mary, and she did not disappoint him. But her words were a total surprise. "*Pikiwisimak*." She spoke in clear concise Cree. "Come Home Now."

"What's wrong?"

"Nothing is wrong. It's time you came home. So come home."

Daniel paused a moment, looked around the room, at the bed that was not his, at the curtains that were not sewn by Mary, at the sterility that infects all rental rooms. He could see his packsack still half-filled and knew his truck was still warm. "Okay, old woman. I'm on my way." Daniel hung up the phone and immediately began to press the buttons.

"Hey Joe. I've got something to take care of back home, be a few days. You guys are not going to need me. I got a feeling Jimmy's on his way to town."

Daniel's instinct was correct. He opened the door of the motel room, his packsack slung over one shoulder, and met Jimmy. The barrel of the .243-calibre rifle pointed directly at Daniel's belly button. He stepped back and Jimmy followed him into the room.

Daniel dropped his pack onto the bed behind him. "What do you want?"

"What do *you* want?" Jimmy emphasized "you" with Cree tradition by pointing at Daniel with his lips. "You're the one been looking for me."

Daniel stood silent. He had no response.

"While you been looking for me, I been watching you. You and Charlie walked right past me. Remember that Beaver lodge you stared at along the road. That was my house. You did not come up and knock. So I come to ask what you want."

Henry was conscripted by Jean to drive her and Zach to the bingo. Gladys declined to join them. She did not particularly enjoy bingo. Anyway her Grandmother had her old friend Zach to keep her company and Gladys was happy to be off the hook. Those two old people would be laughing and teasing all night. Gladys did not want to be the object of the teasing, as she inevitably would be if she went with them.

Kathy Bell worked for years at Robertson's Trading Post before she went into business for herself. She built a beautiful large log store and gas station at the reserve crossroads. A large stylized sign with a Northern landscape proclaimed the building Kathy's Korner.

Henry pulled his Toyota Tundra extended cab truck to the pump. Kathy came out, pulling on lined leather gloves. "Fill?" she asked.

"Yes, please." Henry emphasized the 'please' and unlocked the gas cap cover. As he turned away from the truck he caught sight of Edward coming from the store toward a car on the other side of the pump. "Hey Ed," Henry called across the snow-packed lot.

As Henry and Edward visited, Charles walked up with a determined, serious expression. None of the brothers were surprised by the chance meeting — if it was chance and not something more. Henry and Edward *were* surprised however, when Charles stated, "I just saw Jimmy."

Moments later, Charles, Henry, Edward, Jean and Zach were crowded into Daniel's room in the motel next to Kathy's Korner. Daniel sat in a chair between the bed and the South wall. Jimmy stood on the other side of the bed with the rifle levelled at Daniel's head. The others were arranged across the room as the two groups faced each other.

Daniel was aware of the West wall behind him and the South wall to his left. Cornered. He stared straight ahead, expressionless. He should not have wasted time phoning Joe, or dawdled as he packed his few possessions. Two or three minutes earlier and Daniel would have been well on his way by now.

Daniel's thoughts turned to the .243-calibre rifle pointed at the spot on his temple that now pulsated in steady rhythm. Daniel refused the urge to look. He knew the black hole in the end of the barrel would look back at him, knew that a cartridge waited deep down that black hole, cold brass, lead, explosive and detonator. Daniel knew that at four thousand feet per second the projectile would erupt upon contact with his skull. Rumour had it that he would not hear the sound of the shot. He doubted that rumour. The tiny black hole was less than four feet from his temple. The pulsations intensified. Now they sounded with cracks.

The Riverside Motel and Kathy's Korner both back upon the Montreal River. One of Daniel's reasons for choosing that motel was the comforting sound of the river as it passed through a small rapid before flowing out into a bay of Lac La Ronge. *Kitsaki*, or in English, River Mouth, was the name given to the whole area including the bay, but once referred only to the group of houses across the highway from Kathy's Korner.

The river flowed silent this night as the sky cleared and the temperature dropped. The rapid was mostly frozen over and covered by a thick, sound-muffling depth of snow. Perhaps the colder temperature affected the viscosity of the water or more likely the river fell silent because she was there.

She was back in human form, smashing river rocks together and catching the sparks on her tongue. She danced slowly, patiently and watched the back of the motel across the river. The rocks crumbled and she ate some of the finer pieces, tossed them in the air and caught them in her mouth like a teenager playing with popcorn. Then she plunged both bare hands into the snow and brought up two more basketball-sized rocks.

Henry broke the silence that was already broken by the crash of rocks. "What the hell is that?"

"It's her," Jimmy spat.

Jean looked at Zach. "Did you bring it?"

"Never leave home without it." Zach patted the small green packsack still slung on one shoulder. The pack was such a permanent part of Zach that it blended into his clothing. Only when he patted it did anyone notice that the pack was where it always was.

"Who's *her*?" Henry asked.

Jean leaned slightly, hoping to see something out the window behind Jimmy. "Something that is not supposed to be. It's not a her; it's an it. Don't worry — Zach can send it back. Right?" She looked toward Uncle Zach.

"She is what I am going to become unless one of you three shoot me through the heart." Jimmy indicated his brothers who stood shoulder to shoulder to the left of the door. Zach and Jean found chairs and sat to the right — the privilege of age to sit during catastrophe.

"What the fuck are you talking about?" Charles reacted with anger. He remembered this morning's promise at the abandoned saw mill, felt himself singled out and hooked by the promise.

"One of my brothers shoots me through the heart and frees my spirit or I become a *Wetiko* like her."

"Why does it have to be through the heart and not, say, the head?" Henry asked.

"How should I answer my brother the lawyer? Because my spirit is frozen inside my heart. If you kill me any other way, I won't be able to go to the otherside." Jimmy tried to patiently explain, but his voice sounded like he was pleading. "I'll be stuck in this world like her and feed on people."

"This is bullshit!" Edward started to step forward from his place in rank between Henry and Charles. Jimmy raised the rifle slightly. It angled down toward the same spot on Daniel's temple. Edward eased back.

"I love you my brothers. I have always loved you and will always love you. You are my blood. If you do not do what I ask you, you will join me in responsibility for many more dead people." Emotion robbed Jimmy's voice, made it weak. He forced his words through a lump in his throat. "I cannot free my spirit by myself. I need your help. The reason I ask you is because you are my brothers. You share the same blood as me."

Henry started to speak. "There has to be some other way."

Jimmy found his strength again. He would not cry or beg. In his final moments he would stand strong. "What way, Henry? Some special plea in court. A conditional discharge, community service?" What?"

"How about insanity? This is crazy," Henry shot back.

"Psychiatrists don't know how to free a frozen spirit." Jimmy found that calm neutral place where he wanted to be. "Could you really see me locked away with her out there? She's going to be in here in another minute and it's going to be too late."

"That thing's not coming in here," Jean declared. "Like I said. It's not supposed to be, and it sure as hell's not going to come in here, or me and your Uncle will give it what for, and it knows it."

At that moment someone knocked, and the door half-opened. Joe McQuay took a quick look around the room and started to back out again.

"May as well stay, Joe." Jimmy smiled. The rifle remained level. "Now we can have a real sentencing circle. The Queen's representative is here."

"Easy, Jimmy. I'm off duty. Just came to talk Daniel there out of going home." Joe shut the door behind him.

"Daniel." Jimmy let the sound of the name slide around in his mouth. "Daniel who?"

"Settee," Daniel answered defiantly.

The rifle remained steady.

"So, Daniel Settee, you still haven't told me what you want."

"He's a relative," Jean interrupted "He's married to my cousin, Mary."

"Listen, Jimmy," Joe used his reasonable voice. "Taking hostages isn't going to help. Why don't you let these people go and you and I will stay here until we figure it all out."

"Nobody's a hostage. You can leave anytime. The only person I'm worried about is this guy here. This Daniel Settee guy. He tracked me and I tracked him. Pretty soon we'll figure out what the hell he wants."

"You mean I can just walk out the door. You won't shoot?"

"Go ahead. Nobody asked you to come here. You don't have to talk Daniel into staying. He's not going anywhere."

Joe turned and reached for the doorknob, slowly opened the door, and very slowly walked out, aware of the centre of his back. A moment later he walked back in. "You invited me to participate in a sentencing circle. So bring it on."

Zach turned to Jean. "What's a sentencing circle?"

Jean shrugged. "Something they made up and blamed on us."

Joe stood in front of the door directly across the room from Jimmy. Jimmy held his entire attention. "Where do we go from here, Jimmy?"

"We decide which of my brothers frees my spirit."

Joe looked to his right at the three brothers, as if for the first time fully aware of their presence. "Tell me."

"He wants one of us to kill him," Charles answered.

"There's a good pistol in the top of my pack and a box of shells in the front pocket," Daniel offered grimly.

"Go ahead." Jimmy indicated the pack at the foot of the bed, pointing with his chin.

Joe stepped forward ahead of Charles. The large canvas bag was a typical trapper's pack with wide leather straps and sturdy buckles. He carefully opened the pack while he kept his eyes on Jimmy. "I won't ask about permits!" Joe removed the pistol and the small box of cartridges. He stood upright and stepped back to the door. He moved with care, caution and calm, placed the pistol in his waistband at the small of his back and the box of cartridges in his pant pocket. The pistol was now as far away from Jimmy as possible with Joe physically between him and it. Joe was the smallest man in the room at five foot eight, yet he dominated it now with his presence.

She shrieked and clawed at the roof.

"What the fuck was that?" Edward looked toward the ceiling.

"It's her." Jimmy's voice sounded weary.

Charles looked past Joe at Zach and Jean. His silent request for an explanation was answered silently by Jean. She simply glanced at the ceiling and slightly shrugged.

"Do you hear that, Jimmy? That's the sound of RCMP special officers. This motel is surrounded. You have no way out. It's okay. They won't come in. They're just taking up positions for now. It is still up to you. We can work this thing out." Joe was unsure of his explanation. It was far too soon after his call for assistance. And, what the hell were those crazy bastards doing shrieking like banshees on the roof. As far as Joe knew it was not part of RCMP training.

"Your friends are not here, yet." Jimmy stated flatly. "It's her. Come on, we don't have a lot of time to fool around." He looked toward his brothers.

"*No.*" Henry's single word hit the room — not loud but definite. "I can't even imagine doing something like that."

"How about you, Edward?" Jimmy's focus shifted.

"I can imagine it. But I don't know if I can do it. Maybe if I'm sure it's the only way." Edward felt the weight of many deaths, his Mother, friends, miners.

Tires crunched snow outside. Heads turned slightly to the sound. There was no need for words. Everyone in the room knew that the police had definitely arrived.

It was now thirty-seven below. Officers felt the clear night air hit them as they swarmed from cars and vans.

"Shoot the crazy fucker in the head." The woman in the white dress yelled and grabbed Inspector Spross' shoulder with both hands. He spun away to break her grip.

"Get this woman out of here," he snapped a command to nearby officers. Spross continued to orchestrate the containment teams. As two officers marched her away she continued to rant: "Shoot him in the head. He's crazy. Shoot him in the head." She whispered into the ears of her escorts and shouted to officers they met. "In the head. Aim for the head."

Joe asked Jimmy, "Can I go out again?"

"Up to you."

Joe left.

"If they kill me," Jimmy spoke slowly, deliberately, "you still have the responsibility to free my spirit."

"How do we do that?" Henry asked. He moved away from the wall slightly, but still stood in rank with his brothers.

"Cremation." Jimmy aimed his words more at Charlie. "Make sure my heart is thawed out."

Charles looked to Uncle Zach for conformation. Zach nodded: "He's right."

"That's not the only way." Jean remembered.

"That's the only way," Jimmy corrected her abruptly. Then he remembered their relationship. "I'm sorry, *Nokom*, but that is the only way." He spoke with as much gentleness as possible.

"I'm coming back in." Joe's words followed his knock on the door before he carefully opened it. He made a show of shutting the door securely. "Everything is under control, Jimmy. We can take as long as we need to work this out. It's all up to you."

"It's up to them." Jimmy nodded toward his brothers. "And it's up to her." He looked at a spot slightly above and behind Joe.

"Who's her?" Joe looked over his shoulder at the white door.

"The *Wetiko* who bit me. The *Wetiko* who is waiting for me. The one who eats trees and rocks and never stops eating."

"I'm not going to argue with you Jimmy. If there is anything I learned these years in the North, it's how much I don't know. If you say there is a *Windigo* out there, that's good enough for me. I don't have to believe in a *Windigo* to accept that you do." "Joe, it's not a matter of belief," Jimmy said. "It's a matter of being eaten."

"Okay." Joe became direct. "So what do you want?"

"What do I want? All I've ever wanted was to live to become an old man. Live out my life and look back."

Jean looked sharply at Zach.

Jimmy continued. "That's not going to happen. I'm not going to see the quiet years. Tonight is my last night."

"Easy, Jimmy." Joe slightly raised his hands, as though he were calming the water.

"Yeah, it's easy to say, Joe. One of my brothers does his duty or your friends out there will eventually charge in here."

"You got it wrong, Jimmy. Those men out there are RCMP. They will not fire unless they absolutely have to. Remember a few years ago. Those two men and a woman who shot the Mountie in Manitoba. Well, when they had them surrounded in a motel, the one fellow came out shooting. Immediately after he was brought down, the officer in charge ordered a cease fire, and went back to negotiation." Joe had moved slightly forward from the door. Now he stood at the foot of the bed and rested one hand on Daniel's pack. "That's what you can expect from well-trained disciplined officers. That's who's outside. You and me Jimmy, we have all the time in the world. No one is going to come charging in here. Those aren't city-cop cowboys out there."

"I killed cops."

"Don't matter who you killed Jimmy. We take it serious when you kill one of us for sure. We can't have that. But it's because our lives are at risk. Those men out there aren't thinking about vengeance. This has nothing to do with revenge."

"What about Albert Johnson?" Edward put in.

"What about Almighty Voice," Zach added.

Joe looked toward Zach. "I never heard of Almighty Voice."

"Before your time," Zach answered. "Oh, your police used cannon on him."

Joe continued to stare, then shrugged and indicated with slightly raised palms and a shake of his head that he did not understand.

"He killed one of his own cows," Zach explained. "It was a long time ago."

"How about you Charles?" Jimmy called upon his little brother. "You said, '*Anything*' this morning."

"And you said I might regret saying it, and I do. I'm into life now, Jimmy. My days of self-destruction are finished. I know something about what you're feeling, though. I know what it feels like to want to go to the otherside, just kick this side and go. I know where you are. I've been there. And honestly," Charles paused as a deep sorrow passed through him. "Honestly, Jim, I can't say which is better, to end it or stay here and keep fighting. I know I couldn't stay here alone. I need you guys a lot more than you know. I don't think I could make it by myself. I hope someday down the road I'll be healthy enough to give back. But today — today, I'm still pretty fucked up. I'm not trying to back down on you, Jim. This isn't self-pity. All I'm saying is that we need each other."

Charles stopped talking. He suddenly felt Jimmy's need, a need as deep as any that Charles had ever experienced. He heaved a long heavy sigh. "Well, give me the gun then." He turned toward Joe.

"Think about it, Charlie." Joe stepped back so that he could face Charlie without taking his eyes off Jimmy.

"What's to think about? You can't rationalize this. It has nothing to do with right and wrong and law and order. It's about my brother being in more pain than the Creator intended a person to handle. I'll just be the instrument that brings that pain to an end. You know the only thing that bothered me about killing myself was knowing it would be a long time until I made it to the otherside, that I would be stuck between this world and that one until my reason for being here in the first place was finished." Charles moved closer to Joe, until they stood only a few feet apart. "Now Jim over there, what's he got? He can't get away and live in the bush forever. She'll get him or the winter will, or maybe they're the same thing. I don't know. If you guys get him you'll either put him in prison or a crazy house, and then what?" Charles was waving his arms around, indicating

Jimmy, then pointing at Joe. "He's going to suffer for a long time then die, and he is never going to get to the otherside." Joe was having trouble keeping an eye on Jimmy and Charles at the same time. "He's going to end up like her and I don't want my brother screaming on the roof of my house or my kid's house or my grandkid's house." Charles was ready. Knew he was ready. He wasn't pitiful Charlie anymore.

"Give him the gun." Daniel felt the throb in his temple; worried that a blood vessel would burst. A stroke would leave him crippled or dead. He watched his life pass, not in a flash, but frame by vivid frame: himself as a child in a time that would never be again, as a young man, full of energy, strong, daring and alert. Mary, Mary giving birth, Mary in the bow of his canoe, the first pair of snowshoes he made, the pile of shavings on the floor of Mary's kitchen. A twelve-point bull Moose, a mere fifty feet away that he did not shoot, lowered his rifle and watched the giant slowly walk away into Pine. A broken leg twenty miles from home, Moses his first dog, his children, his grandchildren, weddings, and funerals.

Daniel realized that he had no regrets. There was nothing he would change, nothing he would do different. Even the mistakes and hard times were part of a good life. If the small black hole erupted now, it would be okay. Daniel understood the ancient cry "It's a good day to die." But not a stroke, not crippled, not bound to a wheel chair. Daniel tried to calm his pounding heart, found he could control his breathing, pace the slow in and out. But the throb in his temple beat its own strong rhythm.

She screamed, shoved an officer so hard that he fell face first into the snow, and ran toward the motel door.

"What the hell! Stop that woman." Inspector Spross' command was not necessary. Two officers sprinted after her. "I thought I said to get her out of here." This was not professional and Spross needed to be professional.

Sergeant Thompson was about to tackle her when she spun around and slashed his face. Her claws ripped through his cheek and nose. The force of the blow snapped his head aside and sent him sprawling. The second officer grabbed her from behind to pin her arms to her sides. She shrugged him off, turned and kicked him in the groin. Before she reached the door a half-dozen officers broke from cover behind cars and converged upon her. Sergeant Thompson charged into the fray, his hands finding a grip on the leather dress. He yanked her back, spun around and threw her to her knees midway between the motel and the nearest police car. She stood up, looked at the contingent of officers between her and the door, at the other officer's careful approach from either side, turned with a shriek and jumped over the police car and fled into the dark.

Inspector Spross felt his anger rise. This was not the way it was supposed to go. He should be inside negotiating, not out here freezing. Fuck it was cold. His toes were numb. An officer approached "Sir, I just heard it's forty-seven below. Request permission to rotate the men. Let some of them warm up in the cars."

"Permission granted, and if that crazy fuckin' woman comes back, shoot her."

"Sir?"

"Just make sure she doesn't come back."

Inspector Spross stood a moment, looked toward the sky, perhaps for help. Stars embedded the black. Even with the streetlights they maintained their brightness. Northern lights streamed, brilliant green tinged with red, across the entire sky. As he watched, the red tinge flared until it dominated, held dominance for a full minute, then gave way till it was just a

HAROLD JOHNSON

tinge on the silver green. The light dance increased its tempo as
Spross found the door handle to the car and warmth.

His moment of anger passed. Spross had to calmly
re-evaluate. His available force would be reduced by at least a
third from the need to keep warm. He thought of moving the
army closer and decided against the move. His containment
teams could handle this. There was no need to share.

"Zachias."

"What?"

"You know what."

"I'm not to interfere, remember."

"Zachias!" Jean's tone threatened.

"You know as well as I do that I have to be asked first."

"He doesn't even know what to ask for, doesn't even know he
has other choices. How can you sit there and say nothing? He's
your nephew."

"I can't change the law, not even for my own son. That's how
everything got screwed up in the first place. I can't interfere. I
have to be asked."

"Then I ask you, Zachias. I ask you to use your gift to help
your nephew."

"And who is going to ask you to use *your* gift, my older
sister?"

"You will."

"And what will we do?"

"You heard him. He said he just wants to live to be an old
man."

Lois looked toward the sky. The cold seeped through her thin
nightgown. She really should have worn her flannel tonight.
Surrounded by silent wind chimes, she stood straight on the
tiny deck that ran the length of the front of her cabin, and faced

174

West, toward La Ronge. The dread she felt before going to bed was gone; it had dissipated in the dark. Lois felt out with her heart, conscious of the motion — she felt the warmth in her chest, felt the motion of her heart seeking outward. The answer came. Henry was all right. Nothing was wrong. She watched the Northern lights dance for a while before the cold forced her back into the warmth of her cabin. She made tea, one bag in a cup, a little milk and sugar. Everything would work out. Now she could sleep peacefully.

Joe McQuay sat in the passenger seat and gave his report to Inspector Spross.

"So you left him in there with three old people!"

"Yes, sir. Elders. Around here elders are respected. They might be able to come up with something. It's worth a try."

"And he has a rifle pointed at the head of one of those elders."

Joe took a moment before he responded. "Yes, sir. He has held that rifle to Daniel's head for the whole time. That situation has not changed. On the plus side, his three brothers were ordered out by the elders at the same time that I was. And as I said, Jimmy was trying to convince his brothers to kill him."

"So what do those elders have in mind?"

"I'm not sure, some sort of ceremony I imagine. The last thing I saw before I left was the Elder Zachias removing a leather bundle from his pack. He was unrolling it when I was finally ordered out. Some of the traditional people up here are secretive about their ceremonies."

The officers rotated between positions of advantage and the warmth of their cars. The night continued cold. The Northern lights waned, then resurged even brighter with more red than before. Hours later the door to the motel room opened and three figures filed out. Joe threw open the car door and was first to the three Elders. Jean and Zach walked past him silently, sternly. The third old, old man Joe did not recognize. "Who's he?" Joe grabbed Zach's sleeve.

"His name is Adolphous." Zach replied.

"Where's Jimmy?"

"Jimmy paid for his sins with most of his life." Jean answered slowly.

Joe looked toward the door of the motel as Daniel emerged. "What happened in there?" He asked his old friend.

"I'll tell you about it another time, Joe. Right now I just want to go home." Daniel looked toward the sky and the flare of Northern lights. He wondered which bits of light were his ancestors. Where in the sky did his Grandfather dance? He reached upward to stretch muscles tired from sitting far too long. He threw his pack in the back of his truck and sat, watching for a minute as the engine warmed up. No sense in driving a truck with a cold engine, just causes unnecessary wear. Mary would be there when he got home no matter how long he took.

Joe cautiously entered the motel room. It was empty. It smelled of smoke. Sage maybe, or Sweetgrass, Joe surmised. The usual smells of ceremonies and something else that Joe did not recognize permeated the room. The window at the back was open slightly and the cold night air had already diluted the smells in the room. Joe ran around to the back of the motel. There were too many tracks under the window to decipher. He asked the shivering officer, "Did anyone come out that window?"

"No, sir. I've been here for at least an hour and a half and the only thing that came out of that window has been smoke."

"Are you absolutely sure? You watched that window for every minute."

"Yes, sir. Every minute?"

Joe shone his flashlight on the ground to look for tracks. There were many, but he could not tell if they might be Jimmy's or the officers'. He couldn't really blame a man for turning away from the wind once in a while. He doubted that a man half-frozen could have watched the window every minute. On a night like tonight, his eyeballs would have froze.

CPSIA information can be obtained at www.ICGtesting.com
Printed in the USA
LVOW11s0721100914

403269LV00001B/4/P